SEALED WITH A KILL

SEALED WITH A KILL

LUCY LAWRENCE

WHEELER
CHIVERS

This Large Print edition is published by Wheeler Publishing, Waterville, Maine, USA and by AudioGO Ltd, Bath, England.
Wheeler Publishing, a part of Gale, Cengage Learning.
Copyright © 2011 by Penguin Group (USA).
The moral right of the author has been asserted.
A Decoupage Mystery.

The text of this Large Print edition is unabridged.
Other aspects of the book may vary from the original edition.
Set in 16 pt. Plantin.

LIBRARY OF CONGRESS CATALOGING-IN-PUBLICATION DATA

Lawrence, Lucy.
  Sealed with a kill / by Lucy Lawrence. — Large print ed.
    p. cm. — (A Decoupage mystery) (Wheeler Publishing large print cozy mystery)
  ISBN-13: 978-1-4104-3943-7
  ISBN-10: 1-4104-3943-7
    1. Decoupage—Fiction. 2. Murder—Investigation—Fiction. 3. Large type books. I. Title.
  PS3612.A948.S43 2011
  813'.6—dc22   2011015482

BRITISH LIBRARY CATALOGUING-IN-PUBLICATION DATA AVAILABLE

Published in 2011 in the U.S. by arrangement with The Berkley Publishing Group, a member of Penguin Group (USA) Inc.
Published in 2012 in the U.K. by arrangement with The Penguin Group USA Inc.

U.K. Hardcover: 978 1 445 83836 6 (Chivers Large Print)
U.K. Softcover: 978 1 445 83837 3 (Camden Large Print)

Printed in the United States of America
1 2 3 4 5 6 7 15 14 13 12 11

For the hooligans, Beckett and Wyatt.
You are my joy.

ACKNOWLEDGMENTS

I just write the books — that's the easy part. The hard work is saved for my agent, Jessica Faust; my editor, Kate Seaver; her assistant editor, Katherine Pelz; the art department for Berkley Prime Crime (best covers ever); and let's not forget the wonderful folks who work at bookstores like the Poisoned Pen. These are the people who help us all find refuge from real life between the covers of a book. Thank you all. Without you, I'd be lost.

CHAPTER 1

"Well, what do we have here?" Ella Porter asked. "Is that Nate Williams, driving with a young woman I've never seen before?"

"It is," Marie Porter, Ella's twin, confirmed.

Brenna Miller reared up from her crouched position at the back of the Jeep and smacked her head on the open hatch door. *Ouch!*

She clapped a hand on her head and turned to follow the directions of the sisters' gazes. Sure enough, Nate's vintage pickup truck was leaving a trail of dust behind it as he roared up the drive toward the communal lot where Brenna was parked.

The trees that lined the road behind him were ripe with the vibrant autumn colors of candy apple red and golden butterscotch. The late-September sun was warm, but the air held a bite of the rapidly approaching New England winter.

Autumn was Brenna's favorite time of year. The sticky humid heat of summer left and took its mosquitoes with it. It was once again cool enough to turn her oven on and do some serious baking without transforming her kitchen into a blast furnace. It was finally cool enough to don her favorite clothes: jeans and sweaters. But the capper was that the World Series would be played, and since she and Nate shared a love of baseball, this meant a lot of TV time together even though they followed different teams — rivals, in fact. Yes, Brenna loved October.

The windows of the truck cab were down, and Brenna saw Nate flash a smile at her as he pulled up beside them. As always, she couldn't help but return his grin. The man was a charmer, for sure.

He climbed out with a wave and circled around to open the door for his companion. The first thing Brenna noticed was that she was young. Her wavy brown hair was styled in a bob, reminiscent of a flapper from the twenties. Her jade green earrings dangled, and she smiled up at Nate as he helped her out of the truck. She carried a bright green shoulder bag and wore a cute yellow dress with a slightly poofy skirt that ended at her knees, very retro.

Brenna couldn't help glancing down at her own holey jeans and baggy sweatshirt. Her shoulder-length auburn hair had escaped its clip and was hanging half in her face. She probably looked like she'd spent the day washing windshields for nickels at the interstate on-ramp on the outskirts of town. Fabulous.

Nate walked over to Brenna and the Porter sisters with the young woman beside him.

"Good afternoon, Brenna, ladies," he said, and he inclined his head.

The twins, who were within bragging rights of reaching their seventieth birthday, twittered beneath his attention, while Brenna said, "Hi, Nate."

"Let me introduce your new neighbor," he said. He gestured behind him. "This is Siobhan Dwyer. She'll be staying in the cabin next to yours for a while. Siobhan, this is Brenna Miller, one of our resident artists. I let Brenna stay here even though she likes the Red Sox, because she makes the best brownies in town."

The Porter sisters glanced between Nate and Brenna with identical looks of speculation. She could only imagine what the two gossips were thinking: that she and Nate were shacking up. She decided she'd better defuse the situation before things became awkward.

A bark interrupted whatever she was about to say as Hank, Nate's golden retriever, came bounding up the hill. He looked as if he hadn't seen Nate in days instead of just hours. Jumping up on his hind legs, he licked Nate's face and then turned to jump on Brenna as well. While she rubbed his ears, Nate retrieved his tennis ball from the grass and threw it back down the hill toward the lake. Hank did a giddy spasm of joy and set out after it with a happy bark.

"You also put up with me because I'm a great dog sitter," Brenna said.

"Hank does adore you," Nate agreed with a smile that crinkled the corners of his eyes and made Brenna hope he wasn't just talking about Hank.

"Well, I guess I know who to see when I want a brownie," Siobhan said, bringing the attention back to herself. "Although, I find too many sweets can ruin a girl's figure. But then at your age, you probably don't have to worry about that."

Brenna blinked, uncertain of whether she'd just been insulted or not. She decided to write it off as a bad attempt at humor.

"Yeah, I'm definitely a grown-up," she said

with a forced chuckle. "Welcome to Morse Point, Siobhan."

She held out her hand. The young woman hesitated and then brushed Brenna's fingers with hers for just the briefest moment. Her fingers were icy cold, and Brenna resisted the urge to rub her hands together to warm them up.

She turned and gestured to the elderly twins. "These ladies are Ella and Marie Porter. We've just gotten back from a furniture salvaging expedition over in Auburn, and they're helping me unload."

Siobhan looked the women up and down but did not offer her hand. "A pleasure."

"Likewise," the sisters said together. They didn't sound very sincere.

"Nate, would you be a love?" Siobhan asked as she ran her hand down his arm and then motioned toward the back of the truck. There were several boxes, an easel, and what appeared to be a stack of canvases. "I'm just exhausted from my trip."

"No problem," he said.

Brenna and the Porters watched as he hefted a few of the boxes and headed down the trail toward the cabin. Siobhan followed behind him, carrying nothing, not even her bright green bag, which she'd left on the ground at their feet.

Brenna wondered if she thought they were going to carry it for her. She looked at Ella and Marie. They had equally put-out expressions on their faces.

"I don't like her," Ella said when Siobhan was out of earshot.

"You don't like anyone," Marie said.

"So?" Ella asked. "That doesn't mean I'm wrong about this one. There's something very cat chomping on a canary about her. I'm only surprised feathers don't fly out of her mouth when she speaks."

"You're exaggerating," Marie said. "What do you think of her, Brenna?"

"Nate must have a reason to be renting to her," she said. Although, privately, she couldn't imagine what it was, since, like Ella, she did not get a warm and fuzzy feeling from the girl.

She watched as Siobhan disappeared into her cabin with a twirl of her skirt. *Sly,* that was the word she brought to mind. Brenna couldn't help but feel that she was the sort of person you didn't turn your back on.

"Oh, lookie here," Ella said from beside Nate's truck. "Paintings, and they're all of her."

She had peeled back the brown paper wrapping from one of the canvases and revealed a portrait that was obviously of Siobhan. It was very Frida Kahlo, a head shot with a severe expression done in bold colors.

"Ella, get away from there," Brenna ordered.

She glanced at the cabin to see if Nate and Siobhan were returning.

Ella leaned in close and said, "The name in the corner is Si-oh-bhan. What kind of name is that?"

"That's her name: Siobhan," Brenna said. She had to hide her smile at Ella's frown. "It's an Irish name pronounced *shiv-awn.*"

"Well, that's just ridiculous," Ella said. "There's no 'v' in her name."

"You're just not as cultured as the rest of us," Marie said. She tipped her head up in a superior look.

"Oh, please," Ella snapped. "You didn't know how to pronounce it, either."

"I most certainly did."

"No, you didn't."

"Yes, I . . ." Marie began to argue, but Brenna cut her off.

"Ladies, can we get back to the task at hand?"

Ella dropped the paper wrapping and curled her lip in distaste. "Well, it seems Miss Siobhan has a very high opinion of herself."

"That's not for us to say," Brenna said.

She turned back to the Jeep and pulled out a drawer from the small dresser she had found in the secondhand shop and handed it to Marie.

"I wonder where she's from," Marie said as she cradled the drawer and headed down the hill toward Brenna's cabin. "She's definitely not from around here."

"How can you tell?" Brenna asked, handing another drawer to Ella before taking the last one herself.

"We'd know her people," Ella said, as if it were obvious.

"You don't know everyone," Brenna said.

"Yes, we do," they said together.

Brenna rolled her eyes. The twins were an information superhighway unto themselves, no doubt, but even they couldn't know everyone in the Morse Point area.

It took the three of them to wrestle the dresser out of the back of the Jeep. They were about to heft it down the hill when Nate came sprinting up to them.

"I'll get that," he said.

Ella and Marie sagged in relief and dropped their end on the ground.

"You don't have to," Brenna said.

Nate just gave her a penetrating stare as he lifted the solid maple bureau out of her arms and made his way down the hill with it.

"So nice to have a man around," Marie sighed.

"Indeed," Ella agreed. "And just look at the way his back muscles bunch — why, I bet he could pick me up with one hand."

Brenna and Marie gave her identical looks of disbelief.

"What?"

Brenna shook her head, refusing to comment. She helped the sisters pack their own treasures from the secondhand store into their Buick and waved as they headed down the dirt drive to the main road.

They departed quickly, as Marie was driving and she was well-known for being heavy footed on the accelerator. Brenna winced and cringed when Marie didn't stop at the end of the drive but hauled that Buick carcass across two lanes and sped toward town. Thankfully, there were no other drivers on the road at the moment.

She perched herself on the open back of her Jeep and played fetch with Hank. She told herself it was because he looked lonely, but she knew better. Her eyes kept straying toward her new neighbor's cabin, and she knew she was waiting for Nate to make an appearance. He had taken the last load of stuff to Siobhan's after he had helped her with her dresser. Not that it was any of her business who this girl was, or why she was here; still, she had no intention of moving until she saw Nate come out of her cabin.

Hank dropped a slobber-covered ball at her feet, and she scooped it up and threw it across the meadow that stretched out behind the row of cabins on the other side of the lake. Hank took off in a flurry of fur, and Brenna headed back to her seat, only to find Nate already sitting there, watching her.

"You spoil him," he said. "I had a perfectly well-behaved dog before you came along."

Brenna scoffed. "Oh, please; I'm the disciplinarian. You're the pushover."

"Ha!" Nate said. "Who lets him eat at the table?"

"*Next* to the table, not *at* it," she corrected. "He has good table manners. And you should talk. Who lets him sleep in the bed with his head on the pillow?"

"He keeps me warm," he argued.

As if he knew he was the object of their conversation, Hank wagged his way over, nudging his head between them, demanding love.

They both obliged, and when their hands collided in his fur, Brenna moved hers to run down his back, wondering if Nate felt the same spark of awareness she felt or if it was all in her head.

"So, a new tenant?" she asked.

"Temporarily," he said. "She's a friend of an old art-school buddy of mine. He e-mailed me last week and asked if she could stay here for a few weeks."

"Oh, so she's not from around here?" Brenna asked.

Nate grinned. "The Porter sisters could tell, eh?"

"Yeah," she confirmed.

"I figured," he said. "Honestly, I don't know much about her. I picked her up at the train depot in Milstead. She'll be here for a bit to do some painting, I'm assuming. She seems nice enough."

"Hmm." Brenna said nothing more.

"So, are you up for the game tonight?" His gray eyes met hers, and as always, Brenna found it impossible to look away.

"I don't know why you put yourself through the torture," she said. "You know the Red Sox are going to spank your sad little Yankees right out of any hope they have to make the play-offs."

"Spoken like a truly deluded member of Red Sox Nation," he said. He rose and stretched his back. "Eight o'clock, my cabin, big screen. Be there."

Brenna grinned. "I'll bring pie. Chocolate cream okay?"

"Oh, yeah," he said. "For chocolate cream, I'll even let you boo my team once."

"Twice," she haggled.

"Once per slice," he countered.

"Deal," she said.

"Oh, and I invited Siobhan to join us," he said. "Since she's new in town and all, it seemed the neighborly thing to do."

Brenna frowned. Nate had never been concerned with being neighborly before.

"That's okay, isn't it?" he asked.

"Oh, yeah — it's great!" she said, forcing a smile. Big, fat lie.

She watched him walk away with Hank at his side, knowing that the ridiculous jealousy she felt meant that the crush she'd had on him for the better part of two years had not diminished one little bit. Darn it. As with the common cold, someone should really have invented a cure for this condition by now.

CHAPTER 2

"I didn't know a vein in the forehead could protrude quite like that," Marie said to Ella. "Do you think he's having a stroke?"

"He's certainly red in the face," Ella agreed. "Maybe it's a heart attack. Should we call someone?"

Brenna Miller glanced up from her sketch pad. She was sketching a decoupage design to put on the dresser she had salvaged. It was scarred and scratched, but given that it was three drawers of solid maple for twenty-five dollars, she considered it a steal. If only she could get the gossip sisters to zip it so she could concentrate.

"Don't you two think you should mind your own business?" she asked as she reached for her steaming latte.

The three of them were sharing a window booth at Stan's Diner. It overlooked Main Street, which was perfect for the twins, the town busybodies, to watch the comings and goings of the residents of Morse Point.

"Brenna, this is Tenley, your best friend, who also happens to be your boss. You have a vested interest in this. In fact, you should be up here with us," Marie said. She never took her eyes away from the window, as if she was afraid she might miss something big.

Brenna half rose from her seat and glanced over the elderly ladies' shoulders. Sure enough, Tenley Morse was outside going nose to nose with her father. Things had been tense between Tenley and her parents ever since she'd opened her specialty paper store, Vintage Papers.

Tenley's parents wanted her to be married to a doctor or lawyer and have 2.5 babies like her three sisters. The young-female-entrepreneur thing she had going was not working for them, so of course their response to Tenley had been to shun her.

For the past two years, although they lived in the same town — Morse Point being named for their family — they seldom crossed paths. And when they did, Tenley was the recipient of the curt nod and the air-kiss. You could feel the love, really.

That was, until today. Surprise, surprise, as they were lunching at Stan's, Mr. Morse happened by and beckoned Tenley outside for a talk. The Porter sisters had taken up residence in the window like a pair of potted plants and had been reporting on the conversation for the past ten minutes.

As Brenna watched, she saw Tenley recoil from something her father said as if he had hit her with a physical blow. Her long blond hair covered her face as she lowered her head in what looked like defeat.

In his early sixties, Mr. Morse was handsome in an all-American-boy-grown-up sort of way. His thick silver hair, which had once been blond, made him look distinguished instead of old, and his eyes were the same striking blue as his daughter's.

He was known about town for his strict adherence to the rules, all rules and any rules. The town code and charter said that littering was punishable by a fine of seventy-five dollars or a night in jail, and when Mr. Morse saw two twelve-year-old boys, Billy Dubbins and Sebastian Martinez, drop their candy wrappers on the sidewalk, he fully expected them to pay the money or do the time. Thankfully, Chief Barker, the head of the local police, was not quite so rigid and only made the boys do litter patrol on the town green as a consequence.

Mr. Morse turned and began to walk away, obviously thinking he had made his point. Tenley called out to him, and he turned back with a glance at his watch, which clearly indicated he had better things to do.

Tenley drew herself up to her full height, an inch or two shorter than that of her father, and tossed her hair back over her shoulders. Even from twenty feet away, Brenna could see pure blue fire shine in her eyes. Uh-oh.

"I hope his suit is flame-retardant," Marie whispered to Ella.

"Yep, because she's about to blast him," Ella agreed.

They were right. Tenley sucked a huge breath into her slender frame, and her mouth started moving and didn't stop for at least five minutes. Her father's eyebrows rose so high on his head that they seemed to merge with his hairline. She punctuated her argument with a pointy finger to her father's chest; then she turned on her heel and stomped toward the diner, giving Brenna and the twins just enough time to clamber out of the window before she arrived.

Brenna watched as Tenley's father strode away, stroking the spot on his chest where she had jabbed him and shaking his head.

"I'm thirty-two years old. I will date

whoever I want, whenever I want, wherever I want," she muttered, and she plopped into their booth with disgust.

"Talk went well?" Brenna asked.

"Humph," Tenley snorted.

"Hi, Tenley." Marybeth DeFalco, Stan's best waitress and biggest gossip, sidled up to their table. "Can I get you anything?"

"She's fine," Marie said, and made a shooing gesture with her hand.

"Yeah, we already had lunch and got her a latte from Stan," Ella agreed.

"If you need anything else," Marybeth said. She looked as if it physically pained her to leave a table where there was the potential for so much good dirt.

"Thank you," Tenley said.

Marie and Ella both glared at Marybeth's retreating figure. She was their main competition for the title of Morse Point's gossip queen. Marybeth was married to Officer DeFalco, one of the town's three police officers, and had access to information that they did not. It chafed.

"He actually asked me to cancel a date with Matt so that I could go out to dinner with him and Mother and some young hotshot executive of his named Brian Steele."

"Really?" Brenna asked. "Why?"

"He didn't say as much, but I got the feeling it's a setup," Tenley said. "Probably I'm the bonus he plans to offer to the young mogul."

"How rude," Ella said, and Marie nodded. "I've known your father since he was in short pants, and I can tell you he's always working an angle."

"And he's cheap," Marie added. "He can squeeze a nickel so tight the buffalo poops."

Tenley burst out laughing, and Marie leaned across the table and patted her hand. "You don't pick your relatives."

"No kidding," Ella agreed, with a sidelong glance at her sister.

"No, but I do get to pick my friends," Tenley said. "And I'm glad I have all of you."

"And you get to pick your boyfriend," Brenna said. "Speaking of which, here he comes."

Tenley sat up straight and smoothed her hair. Her blue eyes shone at the sight of the broad and blond Matt Collins as he shouldered his way into the diner.

"Hello, ladies," Matt said. "Mind if I borrow Tenley?"

The twins jammed themselves back in the window as Tenley and Matt stood outside the diner talking. Brenna turned her attention back to her sketch pad.

The brilliant fall leaves on the two-hundred-year-old maples that surrounded the town green inspired her. She could paint her dresser a moss-colored green and then decoupage autumn-colored paper leaves all over it. Maybe she could even work a dark twisty vine across the drawers from one corner to the other.

"My, isn't he just the handsomest man?" Ella asked.

"He's no John Henry," Marie sniffed. "But he is quite good-looking."

"Humph. What do you know about John Henry?" Ella grumped. "You only had one date with him, and that was over fifty years ago."

"I know that he loved me," Marie said.

"He thought you were me," Ella argued.

"We danced under the stars at the Governor's Ball," Marie sighed. "It was a magical evening."

"It was my magical evening that you stole," Ella fumed.

Brenna had heard the twins squabble over the mysterious John Henry for the past two years. She didn't know whom to believe or which of the two he might have been in love with, but she knew they both thought they were the love of his life. She wondered.

"Whatever happened to John Henry?" she asked.

The sisters exchanged a startled glance and then frowned.

"So, how about those Red Sox?" Ella asked.

They weren't going to tell. Brenna was shocked. Surely they weren't going to withhold this little gem of gossip, were they?

"I heard they've got the Series sewn up," Marie said.

Apparently, they were.

"I can't believe this!" Tenley burst back into the diner. "Matt just canceled our date. He has a meeting at the restaurant that he can't get rescheduled."

Brenna and the twins stared at her.

"Don't you see?" she asked. "Now I have to have dinner with my parents."

"No, you don't," Brenna said. "Just because they asked doesn't mean you have to go."

All three of them gave her a flat stare.

"Okay, I'm assuming I'm wrong," she said. "But I'm not sure why."

Marie patted her hand. "That's all right, dear. It's all that city living you did during your formative years. You forget how small Morse Point is. Believe me, if Tenley doesn't have a date that night, her parents will know."

"Oh, right," Brenna said. "Well, you could always tell them you don't want to."

Again the flat stares.

"You've met my mother, right?" Tenley asked.

"Hmm, sorry," Brenna said.

Tenley shrugged. "It's just dinner."

But it wasn't. They all knew that. It was Tenley being sucked back into the Morse family vacuum like an errant hair ball. It was about being what her parents expected of her and not disappointing them.

"Maybe you can feign an injury," Ella suggested.

"A sprained ankle," Marie offered.

"Emergency appendicitis," Brenna said. "How can they argue with that?"

"And when they come to see me at the hospital . . ." Tenley said.

"Problematic, but not impossible," Brenna said.

"Maybe you could offer up someone in your place," Ella said. "Like Brenna's new neighbor. That would kill two birds with one stone."

"What two birds?" Brenna asked.

"Well, it would get her away from your Nate, and it would get Tenley out of the

29

dinner."

Brenna felt her face grow warm. "He's not my Nate."

Ella narrowed her eyes and said, "But you'd like him to be."

"I . . ." Brenna started to protest, but Ella waved her hand and said, "Don't bother denying it."

Brenna gave Tenley an exasperated look, and she smiled. The Porter sisters could be maddening, especially when they were right.

"Drink up," Marie ordered as she lifted her own mug. "If Stan's latte can't pick you up, nothing can."

The four ladies clinked mugs.

"Brenna!" Preston Kelly, part owner of the Morse Point Inn, pushed through the front doors of the diner and strode toward their booth. "I need you. It's a matter of life and death!"

CHAPTER 3

Brenna blinked at him. Preston was tall and thin, with a shiny dome on top and a short gray fringe around the sides. Over the past few months, he had grown a matching neatly trimmed goatee, which would have given him a hippy sort of casual look except that he always wore stiffly pressed dress shirts with equally starched khakis. So while the top of him looked like a cool cat, the rest of him was as buttoned down as a banker. Right now, however, he looked frazzled.

"Hi, Preston," she said. "Where's the fire?"

"Fire? What? Oh, you," he said. He waved his hand at her attempt at humor. "This is serious. I need a tour guide for my leaf peepers for tomorrow. Gary has a colonoscopy appointment, and I promised I'd take him. You know how he is about doctors. If I don't take him, he'll ditch."

"Can't say as I blame him," Ella said.

"No kidding. Tell him to leave his dignity at the door on that one," Marie agreed.

"How can I help you?" Brenna asked, trying to get the subject back on track.

Preston and his life partner, Gary Carlisle, had owned the inn for more than a decade and were the driving force behind the town's arts council. Brenna appreciated that they always promoted her decoupage work to their guests and had become good friends with them over the past two years.

"Could you take my group on a tour?" Preston asked. He clasped his hands together in a pleading pose. "I was thinking we could include a class at Vintage Papers later in the week to help promote the shop. You could decoupage a project using the leaves you gather."

"I'm not really prepared," Brenna said. "I don't have anything planned."

"You'll come up with something," Tenley interrupted. "This would be a great draw for the shop."

The businesswoman glint was in her eye, and Brenna had a feeling the thought of dinner with her parents was spurring her to put some effort into the shop.

"I suppose we could decoupage some breakfast trays," Brenna said. "We'd have to press the leaves to get the moisture out, but that would make a perfect leafy souvenir."

"I knew I could count on you," Preston said. "I'll bring them up in the shuttle bus and drop them off at your cabin at ten in the morning. There are seven of them."

"But . . ." Brenna started to protest.

"Oh, don't worry," Preston said as he strode away, quickly, as if afraid she'd change her mind. "I already cleared it with Nate."

The door banged shut behind him.

"Why do I feel like I just got shanghaied?" Brenna asked.

"Welcome to the club," Tenley said, and toasted her with her mug.

A small shuttle bus, which looked like it had once been a stubby school bus but was now painted white, bounced up the drive to the communal parking lot that Brenna shared with all of her neighbors.

There were ten cabins in all. Nate rented them out to a mishmash of artists. In addition to Brenna, there were currently three other long-term renters. Paul and Portia Cherry, marrieds who lived in separate cabins because of Paul's snoring, and Twyla, an older woman known to skip in her broomstick skirts across the grass-covered hills.

Brenna enjoyed her neighbors. In the summer they had spent much of their time standing in the cool water of the lake and barbecuing. Twyla was a vegan and she had even gotten Brenna eating soy burgers.

Brenna wondered if the others had met Siobhan yet and, if so, what they thought of her. Her personal jury was still out on the girl.

With a belch of blue smoke, the bus stopped. Preston stepped out of the open door and assisted the leaf peepers down one at a time. From where Brenna was standing, it was a mixed bag of people — young and old, male and female, mostly female. Preston then handed Brenna a very heavy picnic basket.

"Did I mention lunch is included?" he asked.

"No," she said, straining under the weight of the basket.

"Oh, well now you know. Everyone, this is Brenna Miller, your tour guide. See you in four hours."

With another belch of smoke, the bus tore off toward town. Brenna watched it go, feeling that Preston was going to owe her one after this, a big one.

"Well, I'll just put this basket in my cabin, and we'll begin," Brenna said. "Is everyone wearing walking shoes?"

"Duh," an adolescent boy, who looked about thirteen, muttered.

Brenna frowned. He was skinny and freckled, with locks of carrot red hair poking out from under the knit skullcap he wore plastered to his head. The woman beside him had medium-length red hair of the same beta-carotene shade, so Brenna figured she had to be Mom. The woman smiled apologetically at her, which confirmed it.

Aside from these two, there was an older, gray-haired couple decked out in matching Norwegian sweaters and another young couple who appeared to be on a romantic getaway; at least, Brenna assumed as much, as they seemed to be attached at the lip. Another young woman, who appeared to be traveling solo, rounded out their party. She appeared to be in her early twenties, with ash blond hair and wide blue eyes that were just visible behind a pair of large thick glasses. When Brenna met her gaze, she glanced away quickly as if she was too shy to maintain eye contact.

Brenna ducked into her cabin, put the basket on her kitchen counter, and locked the door behind her. The group of seven was milling about the water's edge, admiring the way the lake water reflected the trees' fabulous foliage. Well, the Norwegian sweaters were. The mother and son were deep in a hissed conversation, while the young lovers were busy staring into each other's eyes. Brenna wondered if she'd have to hose them down once they reached the shelter of the trees.

"Perhaps we should introduce ourselves," Brenna said. Aside from being good manners, she figured this would be important if someone fell in the lake; she'd want to call them by name and not just yell, "Hey, you in the sweater, swim over here."

"This is my son, Tommy," the mother said, and the sullen teen interrupted in a voice laden with attitude and said, "I go by Suede now."

The mother heaved a sigh that sounded like the last of her patience being expelled. "Fine, this is Suede, and I'm Leather."

"Mom!" the teen whined. His face darkened five shades deeper than his hair and he snapped, "Her name is Julie."

"Nice to meet you, Julie, Suede," Brenna said. She gave herself big points for saying it and not laughing.

"I'm Jan, and this is my husband, Dan," the female in the Norwegian sweater said.

Brenna smiled at them. Rhyming names, matching sweaters, and short haircuts for their silver heads — even though it was a bit over the top, they were quite cute in their coupledom.

"I'm Lily, and this is Zach," the female half of the lip-lock gushed, never taking her eyes off of her mate.

Brenna guessed them to be in their mid-twenties. They looked like something out of an Abercrombie & Fitch ad; both were skinny with long hair that draped about them like a curtain when they kissed, which was frequently.

"I'm Paula," the lone woman said to no one in particular as she stared at the tips of her plain, brown walking shoes.

"It's nice to meet you all," Brenna said. She slung a canvas messenger bag over her shoulder. "As Preston said, my name is Brenna. We're going to take a hike around the lake today. Later in the week, I'll be teaching a decoupage class at Vintage Papers in town. The leaves you gather today, we'll use for a project then, so please keep an eye out for colorful ones that you might want to use."

The sweaters nodded enthusiastically; the teen looked sullen, the mother resigned, the single girl nonresponsive, and the young lovers oblivious. Fabulous, Brenna thought; this should be fun.

She began walking the path that led along the edge of the lake. As she passed by, the door to Siobhan's cabin banged open and out stepped the young woman. She took in the group before her and frowned.

"What are you doing here?" she demanded.

"Hello to you, too," Brenna said and kept walking. She did not feel the need to explain herself to someone who lacked the basic good manners of a proper greeting.

Siobhan quickly shut her door and hurried down the steps.

"Sorry," she said as she fell into step beside Brenna. "I was just surprised to see such a large group right outside my door."

"Hmm." Brenna supposed she had a point. "Nate lets Preston, from the inn in town, offer walking tours around the lake. Preston couldn't make it today, and he asked me to fill in for him."

"How far are you going?"

"Not far."

"Into the woods?"

"Yes, but staying on the path."

"Oh." Siobhan said nothing more but continued walking beside Brenna.

It occurred to Brenna, after several minutes, that Siobhan had apparently decided to join the tour. Brenna wasn't sure how she felt about this development, but as they rounded the corner and the sweater set, Jan and Dan, began to pepper her with questions about the wildlife of the area, Brenna didn't have much of a chance to think about it.

As they gathered fallen leaves, which Brenna tucked into her bag, she entertained them with the story about the family of skunks that had moved in under her porch last summer. Hank, Nate's golden retriever, was the unfortunate one to discover them when he went sticking his nose where it clearly did not belong and got sprayed. Nate had gotten the local wildlife management office to help relocate the family of skunks. All went well, but it did take several days for the smell to leave the area.

Most of the group laughed; only Suede the surly teen and Siobhan looked disgusted. The teen, Brenna figured, was disgusted by everything; he was, after all, a teen. Siobhan, however, was clearly lacking anything resembling a sense of humor.

The group was taking a leaf-gathering break and had fanned out along the path. Brenna had found a clutch of oval-shaped golden beech leaves. She was sifting through them, picking out the ones that were not already turning brown.

"I'm sorry about Tommy . . . er . . . Suede," Julie said. She crouched down beside Brenna and began to sort through the leaves with her. "He's become so surly since his father and I split up. I don't know who he is anymore. And yet when I look at him, I see the cheerful little redheaded butterball who used to waddle around the house in just a diaper and a cowboy hat, who was fascinated with his toes and used to giggle at butterflies."

Brenna glanced up to see Suede, knit hat low on his brow, ripped jeans, iPod plugged into his ears, leaning up against a nearby tree with a faraway expression on his face.

"Will it help if I tell you it's just a phase?" she asked.

"Yes," Julie said. "It would. Of course, I'd be really grateful if you could tell me the exact date and time he will start to behave like a human being again."

Brenna laughed. She liked Julie. She didn't seem much older than Brenna herself, and with her heart-shaped face and big green eyes, she had an air of fragility that made Brenna feel protective of her. At the same time, when she gazed at her son, there was a strength in her that ran bone deep, and Brenna knew Julie would never let any harm come to Suede. And her patience with him showed her to be a woman with a great capacity to love.

"No such luck," Brenna said. "However, I have a friend who has five boys. And the last time I saw her, she was looking for a new housecleaning service because her current cleaner quit when the boys decided to make a Mentos-and-Sprite volcano in the living room. It worked — too well."

Julie laughed and said, "Hey, I'm feeling better already."

"I thought you might." Brenna glanced up. The rest of the group was getting ahead of them, so she and Julie left their pile and hurried to catch up.

"Is that a bridled sparrow?" Jan asked, nudging Dan with her elbow.

"Can't be," he said. "They never fly this far north."

He pulled a pair of folded binoculars out of his pocket and stopped walking to train them on the tiny little songbird fluttering from branch to branch.

"You know, I think it might be," he said. He stepped off the path in pursuit of the small bird.

"Dan," Brenna whispered. "You need to stay on the path. Nate is very specific about not letting the wildlife be disturbed."

"Just a couple more steps," Dan said. "I've

almost got a solid visual. This would be a real coup to tell our birder club."

Everyone was silent, waiting for Dan's proclamation. Brenna figured she could give him a second before she yanked him back onto the path.

"Oh, my," Dan said. "It's . . ."

Everyone leaned forward, even Suede and Siobhan, who had been the two complaining the loudest during the short hike, to hear if it was indeed the rarely spotted bridled sparrow.

"It's a . . ."

"A what, Dan? A what?" Jan asked. Her voice held an excited trill of anticipation.

Dan lowered the binoculars and turned to look at the group. His face had gone stark white and his eyes were huge. He looked shocked and shaky.

"It's a hand, sticking out of the leaves over there. My God, I think we've found a body."

CHAPTER 4

Lily screamed and clung to Zach. Suede looked like he was torn between hiding behind his mother and going to check out the grisly scene. When it looked like morbid curiosity was going to win, Julie stayed him with a hand on his arm. Brenna saw a fleeting look of relief pass over his face before he covered it with his usual scowl.

"Dan, come away from there," Jan said. "I've watched enough *Law and Order* to know that we shouldn't disturb anything."

Dan looked unconvinced. "Shouldn't we check to see if he's dead?"

Jan fished into her nylon backpack and pulled out her cell phone. "I'm calling nine-one-one."

Brenna felt light-headed. Hadn't she had enough bodies in the past year? Surely there could not be another one. Not here in her own backyard. It had to be a prank. Halloween was coming. Some of the local kids must have planted a fake hand out here as a prank.

"I'll go check it out," she said.

"I'll come with you," Siobhan said.

"Me, too," Paula said.

Brenna was surprised by the show of support. She would have refused them, but honestly, on the off chance it really was a body, she didn't want to do this alone.

The leaves crunched under their feet as they approached the pile Dan indicated. A large fluffy cloud drifted over the sun, blocking its warmth, and Brenna shivered in her hooded sweatshirt.

As they were folded into the crowd of towering maple, oak, and birch trees, Brenna felt her heart thump in her chest. There were several piles of leaves, swept together by the wind and the uneven terrain. She kept her eyes trained on the largest. At ten feet away, it became obvious there was indeed a human hand poking out of the leaves.

Brenna sucked in a breath. This morning's breakfast put up a mutiny in her stomach, but she forced it back down. She was responsible for this tour. She wasn't going to let them down by losing her cool or her breakfast.

She knelt beside the pile and brushed

away some of the debris. She could feel the two women at her back but noticed that neither of them made a move to come closer to the body. Fine.

She pushed aside some of the leaves where she assumed the head would be. A tuft of white hair showed first. That was as far as she got. Now that she was closer, she could see the dark brown stains in the leaves that could only be blood, and could smell the unmistakable stench of death.

She rose to her feet and backed up quickly. She held out her arms and pushed the two women back until all three of them were in full retreat.

"The police are on their way," Jan said.

"Good," Brenna said. "We're going to need them."

"Did you recognize him?" Siobhan asked. Her look was intense as she scrutinized Brenna's face.

"No," Brenna answered. "There really wasn't enough left of his face to identify."

A gasp rippled through the group.

"Let's move back down the path so Chief Barker can see us," Brenna said. She did not add that she wanted to put some space between her and the dead guy. Judging by the speed with which the rest of the group moved, they felt the same way.

No one spoke as they trudged away from the grisly scene. Brenna felt a buzz in her head as if her ears were ringing, and she wondered if she was going into a minor state of shock.

"Not exactly your average bridled sparrow sighting, now was it?" Paula asked as she fell in step beside Brenna.

Brenna glanced at the young woman. It was just the sort of thing Tenley would have said to distract her from the ghastly discovery, and she appreciated the girl's attempt to break the tension.

"No, not exactly," she said.

"I'm from New York City," Paula said. "I live in Brooklyn, actually. I wanted to get away for a while, away from the hustle and bustle, the noise and the crime, and spend some time in the quiet serenity of nature. Pretty ironic, don't you think?"

Brenna didn't know what to say. How to handle a dead body in the middle of a nature hike was just not covered in any of the etiquette manuals her mother had forced her to read as a kid. She was pretty sure even Martha Stewart would be stumped by this one.

"This sort of thing doesn't happen here very often," she said.

She wasn't sure if she was trying to comfort Paula or herself. Either way it was a big fat lie because this was the third body she'd stumbled upon in the past year.

Paula shrugged and retreated into the warmth of her puffy jacket. Brenna couldn't tell what she was thinking behind her thick glasses, but frankly, she wasn't sure she wanted to know. This was the stuff of nightmares.

In what felt like hours but was really just minutes, they heard the crunch of heavy boots headed toward them. Chief Barker, the head of Morse Point's police department, was coming through the woods flanked by his two officers, DeFalco and Meyers.

"Brenna, the call we got, it can't be right," Chief Barker said. "Right?"

"What call did you get?" she asked.

"A body in the woods," he said.

"Sorry, Chief," she said. "It's under that large leaf pile over there."

He rubbed his index finger across his gray mustache; then he nodded. Brenna noticed his shoulders lowered as if in resignation. It had not been an easy year for the Morse Point police.

"You folks wait here and give Officer Meyers your names and where you can be reached," he said. "We'll go check it out."

He pulled some blue crime scene gloves out of his back pocket, as did DeFalco. The two of them made their way over to the leaves, and Brenna noticed they were careful where they stepped so as not to disturb the area.

The tour group watched silently as the men worked. Officer Meyers, a tall black man with very broad shoulders, was new to the force, having been hired just a few months ago. He made his way from person to person, getting their pertinent information and their accounts of what transpired.

He stopped in front of Brenna last. She had seen him around town and knew that given the size of the town and the trajectory of gossip within it, he probably knew that she had already been on the scene for the discovery of two other bodies.

"Ms. Miller, can I ask you a few questions?"

"Of course," she answered. She kept her gaze on Chief Barker, her own curiosity getting the best of her. Did she know the person in the woods? Had he lived in Morse Point? And why was it always her?

"You're in charge of this tour group, correct?"

Brenna forced herself to glance away from the body and focus on Officer Meyers.

"Yes," she said. "Preston Kelly, the owner of the Morse Point Inn, asked me yesterday if I would take the group for him, as he had a schedule conflict."

"Is everyone here accounted for?" he asked.

Brenna glanced around the group. This was everyone she had started out with, so she nodded. "Yes."

"Can you tell me exactly what happened?" he asked.

Brenna did. It was the same story he had already heard eight times, but he made notes on his little pad anyway.

The chief signaled Meyers to join him and DeFalco near the body. They had a hushed conversation in which Meyers nodded quite a bit. The chief then pulled out his cell phone and made a call, while DeFalco squatted next to the body and Meyers returned to the group with a purposeful stride.

"All right, we have enough information for now," he said. "I'm going to escort you back to the parking lot to await your ride back to town."

Brenna glanced at her wristwatch. They would be an hour early, but it couldn't be helped. Maybe she could offer them all lunch from Preston's basket. Although, looking at the shell-shocked group, she doubted any of them were much in the mood for food right now.

Officer Meyers took the lead and led the group out of the woods on the same trail they had come in on.

"Brenna," the chief caught up to her as she was bringing up the rear. "I've got the state medical examiner coming in. Let's try to keep this quiet as long as we can."

"In other words, don't blab to the Porter sisters?"

A small smile flickered across his face. "That's a little more blunt than I was going for, but yeah, that's the general idea."

"Don't worry," she said. "My lips are sealed. Any idea who he is . . . er . . . was?"

"There's not enough left of his face to identify him," he said. "We haven't found any ID on him. This may take a while."

Brenna suppressed a shudder, barely.

"Why here?" she asked. "Why these woods?"

"At a guess I'd say that whoever put him here didn't think he'd be discovered for a while," he said. "They didn't count on a tour group of leaf lovers."

"Well, then we're even, because I sure didn't expect to find anything more than leaves today, either," she said.

She let out a pent-up breath, and Chief Barker patted her on the shoulder.

"It'll be all right," he said. "I promise."

Brenna nodded and then turned and hurried to catch up to the group. They broke through the trees and cut across the meadow to the parking lot beyond. Siobhan turned and disappeared into her cabin without a word. Brenna couldn't really blame her. What could you say after finding a body? Social niceties seemed awkward at best.

She popped into her cabin and grabbed the wicker lunch basket. Other than Suede, who helped himself to three turkey sandwiches and two apples, no one else took anything except bottled water.

They stood awkwardly on the perimeter of the driveway. Brenna noticed that everyone's gazes would stray toward the woods, and then when there was no sign of activity, they would glance quickly away.

Finally, after what seemed like the longest hour of her life, second only to having her head shoved under a freestanding hair dryer at Totally Polished, the only hair salon in Morse Point, the stubby white bus appeared. Preston Kelly popped out of the driver's seat and gave Brenna a wide-eyed glance.

"Is it true?" he asked.

"I'm afraid so," she said. "But the chief wants it kept quiet."

"Sure, you won't hear a peep from me," he said. "Although, I doubt you'll be able to keep these folks from talking. It had to be a horrible shock to them to find a body when they're supposed to be looking at pretty leaves and cute little chipmunks and birdies."

"A bit," Brenna agreed. "See what you can do for damage control, but I don't think the chief can expect this to stay hush-hush for long."

The group filed onto the bus, and Brenna waved as it disappeared down the drive with another burst of blue exhaust.

True to her word, Brenna didn't mention the gruesome find to anyone. In fact, she spent the next hour in her cabin working on decoupage projects for her classes at Vintage Papers.

Luckily, the leaves she'd found, prior to finding the body on their disastrous leaf-peeping hike, had been protected in her messenger bag during the ensuing hullabaloo and were still usable. She pressed them in an old flower press she'd gotten at a rummage sale years ago. When all of the moisture was squeezed out of them and they were nice and flat, they would make some lovely mementos of the pretty autumn foliage that surrounded Morse Point.

She tried not to think about what was happening in the woods now, but it was hard to ignore when the state medical examiner's van arrived in the parking lot and crime scene personnel began to tromp around the lake to the woods beyond.

Brenna had just brewed a batch of chai tea when a knock sounded at her door. Thinking it had to be the chief or one of his officers, she didn't check before she opened it.

When she had first moved here from Boston, that would have been unheard of for her cautious and somewhat paranoid nature. It just showed how rattled she was that she didn't take a peek first.

As she swung the door open, a flash popped in her face, and she squinted and stepped back. Spots swam before her eyes and it was a moment before she recognized Ed Johnson, the scrawny, bald editor of the *Morse Point Courier,* standing on her front porch.

He smelled of stale cigarette smoke and breath mints. He let his camera dangle from a strap around his neck as he held a mini recorder up to her face.

"Is it true you discovered a body in the Morse Point woods?" he asked.

"No comment," Brenna said. She started to swing the door shut, but Ed wedged his foot in it.

"Aw, come on," Ed whined. "This is news. You've got to help me out."

"I did help you out," Brenna said. "Last spring I found you unconscious in an alley. You owe me for that. Now, I said 'no comment,' and I meant it."

"Just tell me this," Ed cajoled. "Do they know who the body is?"

Brenna rolled her eyes. Same old Ed. In his world, the word *no* meant keep rephrasing the question until you get an answer you can use.

"I can't tell you anything," she said. "You really need to talk to the chief."

"I tried," Ed said. "It'd be easier to shuck a pearl out of an oyster with a rusty paper clip. That man is so stingy with his words you'd think they charge him by the syllable. I can't write a feature on 'Mind your own business, Ed.' "

"Who needs to mind their own business?"

Ed and Brenna turned to find Nate standing on the porch.

"Apparently, me," Ed grumbled, and he

stomped off the porch and headed toward his car, which was parked in the lot on the top of the hill.

"What's got his tighty whities in a bunch?" Nate asked.

"You haven't talked to Chief Barker?" Brenna asked.

"No, I just finished giving Hank a bath," he said. "And I have the war wounds to prove it."

Brenna smiled. Hank hated baths. He loved mud puddles, the swamp, and the frigid lake water, but put him in a bathtub with Mr. Bubble and he was a thrashing, flailing, howling drama queen.

"Is he all fluffy soft and sweet smelling?" she asked.

"Yeah, in fact, I'm not letting him out because I know he'll stay out until he finds something dead to roll in."

Brenna blanched.

Nate's laserlike scrutiny caught the look. "What? Was that too descriptive?"

"No, it's just . . ." Brenna's voice trailed off. "Follow me."

She led the way to the end of her porch, where they could see the parking lot. She pointed up at the medical examiner's van and the two police cars.

"What the heck?" Nate's eyes widened.

"What's going on?"

"I'm not supposed to say," Brenna said. "But since it's your property and all . . ."

"Spill it," he said.

"Okay, when I took that tour group of Preston's around the lake this morning, we found a body half-buried in a pile of leaves."

Nate stared at her until she felt the need to shift her feet to break his gaze.

"Aren't you going to say anything?" she asked.

"I'm speechless," he said. He leaned against the porch railing. "What is this, the third body in less than a year?"

Brenna nodded. "I'm beginning to think I'm a body magnet." She forced a laugh, which Nate did not return.

"Who is . . . was it?" he asked.

"I don't know," she said. She remembered the sight of the blood-encrusted hair, and a shudder rippled through her from her head to her feet.

Nate opened his arms wide, and she stepped into his comforting warmth. He held her tightly against his chest, as if he could keep her safe even from the images burned in her mind.

"Chief Barker asked me to try and keep it quiet," she said.

"I wish him luck with that," Nate said. He

ran his hand up and down the length of her back, and it soothed. "I would be shocked if the Porter sisters don't already know about this, and I'd bet my large-screen TV that they're on their way here right now."

As if his words had summoned them, a large Buick sedan lurched into the driveway. Brenna knew it was Marie behind the wheel as she sped into the lot, narrowly missing the chief's car and then overcorrecting and just whistling by the medical examiner's van by a breath.

The car braked with a jolt. Brenna stepped away from Nate as the two sisters piled out of the car, not even bothering to shut their doors as they scurried down the hill to get to her.

CHAPTER 5

"Looks like you get to keep your TV," Brenna said.

"Whew, the World Series is starting soon," he said.

Brenna could tell that the Porter twins had recently been to Totally Polished and spent some time under Ruby's dryers. Their matching gray hair was styled in freshly tightened curls all over their heads.

It was impossible to ignore them when their tennies churned up turf as they hustled across the lawn, wearing lined Windbreakers over matching nylon pants, Ella in canary yellow and Marie in kelly green.

They stopped, panting for breath, at the base of Brenna's stairs.

"We . . ." Ella gasped.

"Heard . . ." Marie added.

"Body . . ." Ella concluded.

Brenna looked at Nate. He shrugged. It wasn't as if the sisters weren't going to find out what was going on soon enough. Still, the chief had asked her to keep it on the down-low.

Abruptly, it became a nonissue as a team of crime scene personnel broke through the trees, carrying a body bag on the stretcher between them.

"Oh, my . . ." Marie said. She covered her mouth with her right hand and grasped Ella's arm with her left.

"Who is it?" Ella sent Brenna a piercing glance. "And don't tell me that you don't know."

"I don't know," Brenna said.

The elderly twins turned to Nate, who raised his hands in a gesture of innocence or ignorance or both.

"I wasn't there when they found him," he said.

They let out a humph, which seemed to convey how useless they found both Brenna and Nate.

"Oh, there's Chief Barker," Ella said.

"Let's go ask him," Marie said.

Brenna would have told them not to bother, but that would be like trying to catch lightning in a bottle: potentially explosive.

The two sisters trotted off in the direction of the chief, who seemed to be in a deep conversation with the medical examiner. He was tugging at his mustache, an indicator that he was not happy.

"Think we should take cover?" Nate asked.

Brenna hurried across the porch to her front door and opened it wide. "After you."

They slipped inside and closed the door behind them. Brenna closed the blinds so that they could peer out without being seen.

Chief Barker looked like he was ready to growl at the Porter sisters. Brenna saw him shake his head. Marie fluttered her eyelids flirtatiously at him, but when that didn't work, it looked like Ella went for the tough talk. Chief Barker raised one gray eyebrow and gave her a hard stare. The twins walked away, looking dejected at the lack of information.

"Well, it looks like they've been stopped short," Nate said.

"Better the chief than me," Brenna said. The autumn day had turned chilly and overcast. "I made some chai before Ed Johnson showed up; would you like some?"

"That sounds nice," he said. "And you know what goes really well with tea?"

"Hmm, let me guess — brownies?" she asked.

They walked over to the spacious kitchenette on the far side of her cabin. Brenna poured them each a mug and put the honey out. While Nate took over spooning the honey, she got two plates and her Tupperware tub full of brownies, which she'd baked the night before.

"Are these the brownies with the chocolate chunks in them?" he asked.

"Yes."

"Excellent; those are my favorites."

"Are you my friend just for my baked goods?" she asked as she slid a plate in front of him and handed him a fork. She was only partially kidding, but he didn't need to know that.

"Well, that, among other things," he said.

His gray gaze was steady on hers until Brenna forced herself to look away or risk dropping her brownie.

They ate silently, and although Brenna knew that emotional eating wasn't recommended, she couldn't deny that she felt better with a mug of hot tea and a gooey brownie inside of her.

When Nate finished his third brownie, he gathered their plates and rinsed them in the sink.

"I'm going to have to walk Hank for an hour to get that sugar out of my system," he said. "But it was worth it."

He wandered back to the window to watch what was happening outside.

"Uh-oh," he said. "That can't be good."

"What?"

He was staring toward the communal parking lot, so she hurried to join him by the window.

A team of crime personnel were huddled with Chief Barker and his officers on one side of the van. The body had been placed inside and was visible through the open doors at the back. At least, it was visible until a woman in a canary yellow Windbreaker and matching pants blocked Nate and Brenna's view.

"Oh, no, she wouldn't," she said.

"Uh, yeah, she would," he said.

Sure enough, while Ella stealthily crept up next to the body bag inside the van, Marie was moving her Buick out of the way and making a great show of it as she lurched toward the crowd of investigators, sending them scattering.

She rounded the other side of the van just as Ella hopped out of the back. They would have made their getaway, too, except Marie clipped the curb with her right front tire, and with a loud bang and a whoosh of air the tire went flat.

"Should we go and assist?" Brenna asked.

"I suppose it would be the neighborly thing to do," Nate agreed.

Together they trudged up the hill toward the parking lot. Chief Barker looked like he was hanging on to his temper by a mustache hair. The crime scene personnel had climbed into their vehicles and were headed down the drive on their way to the state medical examiner's facility.

Officers DeFalco and Meyers were sharing a car. They made to help the Porter sisters with their tire, but Nate waved them away.

"I'll take care of it; you guys have enough on your plate," he said.

Chief Barker nodded at the men, and they took off in their patrol car with a thanks and a wave.

Marie popped the trunk on the Buick, and Nate pulled out the spare and the jack.

Ella looked at the chief and said, "They're not going to tell Lester's widow, are they? Don't you think that should come from you?"

Chief Barker fixed her with a glare and barked, "What did you say?"

Ella's eyes went wide. Marie fidgeted beside her twin. "I told you not to say anything."

"Well, I just assumed they knew who he

was but couldn't say anything until after they told Lydia," Ella snapped.

Chief Barker took a steadying breath and spoke with a deceptively soft voice. "Explain yourselves, ladies. Who do you think the body is?"

"It's Harvey Lester," Ella said. "Anyone could tell you that."

"And how exactly do you know this?" Chief Barker asked. "Correct me if I'm wrong, but you weren't on the hike today. Was she on the hike today, Brenna?"

Feeling like a snitch, Brenna hedged, "Well . . . uh . . ."

"I thought not," Chief Barker said. "So, how is it, Miss Porter, that you know the identity of that body?"

"It was only a little peek," Ella sniffed. "Not really worth mentioning."

"When?" Chief Barker's face was becoming redder by the second. "Do not tell me it was while your sister was trying to run us down?"

"That was an accident," Marie said. "I got confused between the brake and the gas. It happens all the time."

Chief Barker smacked his hand against his forehead.

"Why didn't I retire last year? I could have retired, gotten a nice package, and I could be fishing now, but no, I decided to stay. I need to have my head examined."

He didn't seem to be talking to anyone in particular, so while Nate worked on changing the tire, the three ladies watched him pace and mutter to himself. When he finally seemed to run out of steam, he turned to Ella.

"So, how do you know it was Harvey Lester? It's not like he had much left to identify."

"Sure he did," she said. "That man's had a birthmark in the shape of a corncob on his neck since the day he was born. Right under his right ear and about two inches long; you can't miss it. And if that isn't enough, he hasn't been to the club in over a week. I was just saying to Marie the other day . . ."

"No, I said to you . . ." Marie interrupted.

"No, I am quite positive that it was me who said to you . . ."

"Sister, you are mistaken. I remember distinctly seeing Mrs. Lester alone again at the bar and saying to you that it was odd not to see Mr. Lester with her."

Ella looked like she was going to wind up and continue the argument. Mercifully, the chief cut her off.

"I want the two of you to give formal

statements at the station immediately," he said. "Do not stop at the beauty parlor, the post office, or Stan's Diner. Am I clear? You are to travel in a direct line from here to the station."

Nate put their flat tire into the trunk and slammed it shut. Both Marie and Ella looked quite pleased with themselves and their roles as official body identifiers.

"We'll see you at the shop," Ella called to Brenna. Then she glanced at the chief. "Later."

"Thank you ever so much for your help with our tire, Nate," Marie said. She gave him her best closed-lipped, coquettish smile.

"Anytime," he said. Brenna could see his lips twitch as he tried not to laugh.

The sisters fell in line behind the chief's car, leaving the parking lot quiet for the first time all day.

"Better them than me," Brenna said. "I can honestly say, this time, this body has nothing to do with me."

"Except that you found it," Nate said.

"Well, except for that," she agreed.

"And except for the fact that Harvey Lester is Rupert Morse's business partner," he said.

Brenna slowly turned to face him. "What?"

"Lester and Morse," Nate said. "Tenley's father, Rupert Morse, has been partners with Harvey Lester for over forty years."

"No, it has to be a different Lester," Brenna said. "And that's assuming the Porter sisters are right. I mean, a corncob birthmark — why, anyone could have that, right?"

Nate just looked at her, his eyes soft with sympathy.

"They're right, aren't they?" she asked.

"The Porter sisters know Morse Point and its residents better than they know themselves," he said. "Still, there's always the outside chance that they could be wrong."

Brenna sighed and turned to admire the lake with all of the glorious autumn foliage circling it like a tiara on a beauty queen's head.

"I should probably go talk to Tenley. She may want to be the one to tell her dad. This is going to be horrible news for him."

"Unless he's the one who did it," Nate said.

"You have been watching too much *Masterpiece Mystery*," Brenna chided him. "Rupert Morse a murderer? That man is as straight-laced as they come. I don't think he could go without wearing his seat belt without hyperventilating, never mind commit murder."

"People have layers," Nate said. "You never know what is going on inside someone's head. All that rule following might have made him snap."

"And he murdered his partner of forty years?" Brenna asked. "No more *Inspector Lewis* for you."

Nate began to walk down the hill toward the cabins, and Brenna followed. "I'm just saying, you never know what lengths even the most law-abiding citizen will go to when they feel threatened."

"Hmm." Brenna refused to comment further. She was not overly fond of Mr. Morse because he was so stiffly disapproving of Tenley's desire to own her own business. Still, a murderer? She just couldn't believe it.

Nate reached out and caught her by the elbow. His gray gaze was intent on hers.

"Promise me you'll be careful," he said.

Brenna felt her throat go dry. She coughed to clear it and said, "Of course. I mean, really, this has nothing to do with me, right?"

Nate let her go with a look of concern, and Brenna tried not to analyze it too much. They were friends. Friends worried about each other. There was no reason for her insides to get all fluttery like that. Really.

CHAPTER 6

Brenna had just shut the door behind Nate when her phone rang. It was Tenley.

"Can you come to the shop right now?" Tenley asked without even saying hello.

"Sure," Brenna said.

She could tell by the high pitch of Tenley's voice that all was not well. Had the Porter sisters stopped by the shop and told her about Mr. Lester? She was surprised they would go against Chief Barker's direct order.

"Did Marie and Ella stop by?" she asked.

"No, I haven't seen them."

"Oh. Are you all right?" Brenna asked. She wanted to give Tenley the opportunity to talk if she needed it.

"Absolutely. Why? What makes you ask?" Tenley's voice sounded guarded.

"Uh, no reason," Brenna said. If Tenley didn't know about Harvey Lester, Brenna didn't want to tell her the news over the phone. "I'll be there in five."

"Thanks," Tenley said with a rush of relief. "I owe you a day off."

"No worries."

Brenna tied her auburn hair back with a ribbon, grabbed her jacket and her keys, and shot out the door.

The drive into the center of Morse Point was a short one. She turned onto Main Street and then took a right into the alley access road that led to the back of the shop. She parked her Jeep behind Vintage Papers and hurried through the back door.

Tenley was just ringing up a sale to Mrs. Huwiler. She had ordered invitations for her husband's retirement party set for next month at the Elks' Lodge.

As soon as Tenley saw Brenna, she grabbed her purse from under the counter, and like a runner passing the baton, she raced out the back door with a faint "See you later" called over her shoulder.

Mrs. Huwiler and Brenna exchanged bemused glances. Brenna forced her lips into a smile.

"Have a nice day," she said.

"You, too," Mrs. Huwiler returned, still looking confused.

Brenna kept busy in the shop. She had been working on a new window display showcasing their new autumn papers. They had just received a batch of handmade papers from a paper craftsman in Ohio. They were rich cinnamon browns, saffron yellows, and pumpkin oranges. She threw in some eggplant purple sheets and then placed fat pillar candles surrounded by multicolored gourds and a garland of autumn leaves around the featured papers, and then went out on the street to examine her handiwork.

It made her fingers itch to do some cutting and pasting. She had just been commissioned by the owner of the Willow House to decoupage four round wooden bar-stools, and she couldn't wait to get started. They were plain wooden stools that she would paint with a base coat of black. The customer had selected some vintage papers that had guitars on them. She was going to cover the seats with cutouts of classic electric guitars such as Fender, Gibson, and Gretsch, and then seal them with heavy coats of polyurethane. They would live in the bar at the Willow House, a coffeehouse and bar on the edge of town. Brenna was hoping that if the owner liked them enough, he'd commission more from her.

Since the shop was in a midafternoon lull, she pulled out her working folder, an

X-Acto Knife, and her cutting board. She sat at the worktable in the back of the shop, slicing the guitars out of the large sheets of paper and fretting about finding a body in the woods, which brought her right back to wondering where Tenley had dashed off to so suddenly.

Brenna wondered if she should have told Tenley about Lester before she hurried out of the shop. What if someone else told her? Then again, maybe that was for the best, since Brenna wasn't sure how you worked "I found your father's business partner dead in the woods" into a conversation.

She didn't know much about Lester and Morse the company. Tenley had once said something about electronic imports, but since she and her family were not presently close, she didn't talk about them very much, and Brenna didn't like to bring up what she knew was a sore subject.

She had just finished cutting out her fifth guitar when the front door opened, letting in a rush of chilly air as the Porter sisters pushed their way toward her table at the back of the shop.

"Is Tenley here?" Marie asked.

"I didn't see her car out front," Ella said. "And she wasn't at the police station, either."

"Why would Tenley be at the police station?" Brenna asked. She put the safety cover on her knife and gathered up her cutouts and papers.

"Well, I would think she'd want to support her father," Ella said.

"I know they don't always get on, but still . . ." Marie added.

"What's going on?" Brenna asked.

"Chief Barker has brought Rupert Morse in for questioning in the murder of Harvey Lester," they said together.

A crash sounded from the break room, and they spun around to see Tenley standing in the doorway.

"Tenley!" Brenna jumped from her seat and hurried across the room. Tenley's long denim skirt sported coffee stains where it had splashed her. A broken mug lay in shards on the floor as the dark coffee pooled in the doorway.

"My father is being questioned by the police?" Tenley asked. "Harvey Lester has been murdered? I don't understand."

Brenna grabbed a dish towel and placed it on the mess. Then she handed Tenley a wad of paper towels to dab at her skirt.

"I didn't get a chance to tell you earlier," Brenna said. "And I wasn't sure if you already knew, but now I'm guessing that you didn't."

"Know what?"

"Harvey Lester was shot dead in the woods," Ella said.

Tenley gasped, and Marie gave Ella a sharp elbow to the ribs. "Way to soft-pedal it, Sis."

"What?" Ella asked. "It's the truth, isn't it?"

Brenna gave them both a stern look.

"You remember the leaf peepers I took around the lake this morning?" Brenna asked, and Tenley nodded. She still clutched the wad of paper towels but had made no move to blot her skirt. "Well, when we rounded the far bend that leads farther into the woods, one of them spotted a hand poking out of a pile of leaves."

Tenley's blue eyes went wide and she covered her mouth with her hand.

"I checked to make sure he was dead," Brenna said. She only blanched a little when she added, "He was, so we called the police, and Chief Barker and the state crime lab came out."

"We identified him," Marie added.

"We?" Ella groused. "You mean me."

"I helped," Marie protested.

"Enough, you two," Brenna said, cutting off what was undoubtedly going to be another squabble between the elderly siblings.

"Why didn't you tell me?" Tenley asked Brenna.

"You were in such a hurry," Brenna said. "I really didn't get the chance."

"I did run out pretty quickly. I had a sudden appointment," Tenley said with a nod. "Sorry about that. I just can't believe this. Who would kill Uncle Harvey?"

"Well, the police seem to think your father had a pretty good motive," Ella said.

"But that's ridiculous," Tenley said. "My father would never harm Uncle Harvey."

"Well, they must have some questions for him," Marie said in a much gentler tone. "They were bringing him in as we were leaving."

Tenley dropped the wad of paper towels on the counter and stepped over the spilled coffee.

"Brenna, would you . . . ?" she asked, but Brenna interrupted with, "Of course, go!"

The Porter twins and Brenna watched Tenley race out the front door and across the town green toward the police station. The wind was blowing, and stray leaves pelted her as the wind tossed her long blond hair around her face.

"Poor thing." Ella *tsk*ed. "Her own father

a murderer."

Brenna gave her a narrow-eyed glance. "Don't start. He is innocent until proven guilty. We don't know anything more than that."

Ella gave her a dubious look but said nothing more.

She and Marie stored their purses in a cupboard in the break room. Marie went to sweep up the shards from the mug while Ella cleaned up the spilled coffee. Obviously, they were planning to stay and help Brenna whether she wanted them to or not.

"I wonder if Lydia Lester knows yet?" Marie asked.

"You'd think the chief would tell her first," Ella said. "I mean, if her husband's business partner . . ."

"Don't start spreading any rumors about Mr. Morse," Brenna interrupted. "You have no idea why Chief Barker wants to talk to him."

The sisters exchanged a glance, and despite her better judgment, Brenna was sucked in.

"What do you know?" she asked.

They gave her matching self-satisfied smiles. When it came to gossip, the elderly twins were more cut-throat than dueling bidders on eBay. Brenna knew she was going to have to pony up some dirt if she wanted the skinny on Lester and Morse.

"Fine, don't tell me," she said.

She tried to play it cool, as if she didn't care. She'd done this dance with the sisters before, after all. The racks of specialty papers needed straightening, so she led the way to the wall where she began to neaten the racks.

The two sisters followed, as Brenna knew they would, and the three of them worked silently. It was a test of wills to see who would crack first.

The only sound in the shop besides the shuffling of paper was the ticktock of the wall clock, marking the minutes since Tenley had left, since her father had been brought in for questioning, since Brenna had found the body.

"Oh, all right," she said. She shoved the last handful of paper into the rack. "I give. What do you want to know?"

Marie and Ella exchanged an awkward high five. First they missed each other's hands completely, and then Ella tried to make up for it with a little too much oomph, causing Marie to wince when their hands smacked. Brenna shook her head.

Ella turned to face her and said, "First

tell us what's going on between you and Nate Williams."

CHAPTER 7

"No!" Marie cried. "That's not what we want to know. We want to know what's happening between her and Dom Cappicola."

"No, we don't."

"Yes, we do," Marie insisted. "I mean, Nate is handsome and all, but Dom is positively magnetic."

"He's a mobster," Ella protested.

"Actually, he is trying to turn the family business legit," Brenna said, feeling the need to defend her friend.

"See?" Marie said. "Now, I know you went on a date with him a few months ago, and I've seen you meet him for coffee at the Willow House, so are you dating?"

"No," Brenna said. "We're just friends."

She didn't feel the need to add the information that Dom would like to be more than friends and that she would happily date him if it weren't for the fact that she had a dead-end crush on Nate. No, that humiliating information was not for public consumption.

"Excuse me," Ella said. "Who was the one who climbed into the van with the dead body? Oh, yeah, that would be me. I get to ask the questions."

"Marie already asked, and I answered," Brenna said. "Now tell me what you know."

Ella looked ready to balk, but Marie chimed in, "I still think you should date Dom."

Brenna gave her a dark look.

"Okay, okay," she said. Marie walked across the room and sat at the worktable. Brenna took the seat across from her while Ella sat on her right.

"Now, we got this from a very reliable source," Marie said.

"Polly Evans, the cashier at the grocery store, heard it from Bonnie Jeffries at the post office," Ella said.

"Who heard it from Tyler Markham, who works in the accounting department at Lester and Morse," Marie added.

"There has been talk at the company that Lester wanted out," Ella concluded.

Brenna waited, but they said nothing further. "That's it?"

"I think that's a lot," Ella huffed.

"Absolutely," Marie said. "If Harvey

Lester wanted out, and Rupert Morse couldn't afford to buy him out, then maybe Rupert got desperate."

"And murdered him," Ella said.

"Or hired someone to murder him," Marie said.

"You should ask that boyfriend of yours, the mobster," Ella said. "Maybe he knows the triggerman."

Brenna had to fight to keep her eyes from rolling back into her head. "He's not my boyfriend and he doesn't know any triggermen."

The twins gave her the same dubious look.

"Well, at least I don't think he knows any," she said.

The door opened and Brenna put on her greet-the-customer face, but it slipped away when she took in a pale, red-eyed Tenley.

The twins hopped up from their seats.

"I'll make some tea," Ella said.

"I'll get some cookies," Marie offered.

In a rare showing of compassion and tact, they left Brenna alone with Tenley to comfort her. Brenna had no doubt that they had their ears pressed to the door, but still she appreciated that they'd vacated the area.

"Are you okay?" she asked as Tenley collapsed into one of the chairs at the table.

"Let's just say that today has not been one

of my best," she said. "Uncle Harvey is dead, they've taken my father in for questioning, and I . . ."

Tenley's voice broke and Brenna draped her arm around her shoulders. She wondered what Tenley had been about to say but she didn't want to grill her.

"Is your mom with him?" Brenna asked.

"Yes, Tricia Morse is trying to work her charm on Chief Barker. It's not really taking," Tenley said. "My sister Carrie is with them."

"She's the oldest, the bossy one, right?" Brenna asked. Tenley gave her a small smile.

"Yeah, she was telling my father not to lawyer up. Apparently, she watches a lot of court TV and feels that she is adequate legal counsel at this juncture."

Brenna felt her lips twitch. She tried to swallow it, truly she did, but the laugh escaped and she was powerless to stop it. Tenley took one look at her and a chuckle erupted from her as well.

It was probably part hysterics from finding a body on Brenna's part and part hysterics at having the body belong to a longtime family friend on Tenley's part, but whatever the reason, they laughed until the Porter sisters reappeared with tea and cookies and gave them reproachful stares.

"Sorry," Tenley snorted. "I'm just a teeny bit hysterical."

"Well, I should think so," Ella said. "A Morse, a member of Morse Point's founding family, suspected of murder, well, it's unconscionable."

Tenley abruptly sobered up. "My father didn't murder anyone. I've heard the rumors that Uncle Harvey wanted out, but you know my father. He's the straightest arrow I've ever known. He and Uncle Harvey would have worked something out. I'm sure of it."

Marie and Ella were silent. Brenna didn't know what to say. In the past few months, two people that she never would have thought were capable of murder had done just that. She was beginning to think you never really knew what a person was capable of when they became desperate.

As if their silence condemned her father, Tenley turned pleading eyes to Brenna. "You'll help me, won't you?"

"Of course," Brenna said. "I'll do anything to help. I can watch the shop while you and your family get through this, and I can bake you up some comfort food. I'm known for my baked goods, after all."

Tenley gave her a watery smile. "Actually, I was thinking more along the lines of you helping me find Uncle Harvey's killer."

"Oh." Brenna blew out a surprised breath. "Okay."

"Oh, thank you, Brenna," Tenley cried and reached across the table to lock her in a tight hug.

"I wonder how Dom is going to feel about you putting yourself at risk again," Marie said to Brenna.

"Never mind him; what about Nate?" Ella asked. "He is going to forbid it."

Brenna let go of Tenley and raised her eyebrows. "I don't see where either one of them has any say in the matter."

Marie and Ella exchanged a glance. It was a sneaky look and before Brenna could say buttinsky, the two of them shot out of their chairs and headed for the door, leaving nothing behind but the scent of Chanel No. 5 and the sound of the jangling bells hanging on the door.

"That can't be good," Tenley said.

Brenna was driving back to her cabin when her cell phone chimed in her purse. She pulled into the lot and fished it out. The number was Dom Cappicola's. Hmm.

"Hello," she answered.

"Please tell me that I heard wrong and that you did not find a body in the woods this morning," Dom said. His deep voice was made even richer, as it was laced with concern, and Brenna wished not for the first time that she was free to like him as much as she was pretty sure he liked her.

Out of habit, she glanced up at Nate's cabin and was surprised to find him standing on the porch with Hank. He raised his hand in greeting and began striding across the lawn toward her.

"Brenna, are you there?" Dom's voice buzzed in her ear.

"Okay, I won't tell you," she said, forcing her attention back to the conversation at hand.

"Oh, man, at least tell me you're not a suspect," he said.

"I'm not!" she said. "Isn't that great?"

"But . . ." he prompted.

Brenna glanced up. Nate was halfway here. She needed to wrap this up.

Speaking very fast in the hope that he couldn't catch every word, she said, "But Tenley's father is a suspect, and she's asked me to help her find the real killer. Okay, I'm driving into a tunnel now — gotta go, bye."

She closed her phone and shut it down in case he tried to call back. She would call him later and explain everything in more detail, but for now she had her landlord,

86

who was frowning at her, to deal with.

She opened the door to her Jeep and was greeted by Hank, who was standing on his hind legs while he tried to lick every bit of her face that he could reach.

"Good boy, Hank," she said. She ruffled his ears, and Nate handed her a soggy tennis ball, which she tossed down the hill. Hank did a double-toe-loop leap of glee and set off after it.

Brenna wiped her face with her sleeve, aware that Nate was still giving her his unhappy face.

"What?" she asked. "Is my rent overdue?"

"You know that's not it," he said. "What's this I hear that you and Tenley are going to look into the murder of Harvey Lester?"

"How did you . . . Have you been talking to the Porter sisters?"

"I went into town to return a library book, and Lillian Page told me that Sarah Buttercomb said that you and Tenley were going to try to clear her father."

"Since when have you been on such good terms with Lillian?"

"She always saves the latest Robert Crais novel for me," he said. "We were just making idle chitchat and . . ."

"And it just happened to turn into a conversation about the body in the woods and Tenley and me."

"Well, the body in the woods is news all over town," he said. "So, it's really not that surprising that we'd be talking about it."

"No, I suppose not," she agreed.

Hank bounded back with the ball in his mouth and dropped it at Nate's feet. He threw it overhand much farther than Brenna ever could, and Hank bolted after it, kicking up leaves and grass in his wake.

"Is it true?" Nate asked.

"Is what true?" Brenna asked, stalling.

"You know what," he said.

"That Tenley and I are going to try to clear her father?" Brenna shouldered her purse and started walking down the hill toward her cabin. "Yes, it's true."

"I don't like this," he said. He fell into step beside her. "Not one little bit. Chief Barker is a good man, and he'll find the killer. You and Tenley need to stay out of it."

"She's my best friend," Brenna said as she stepped up onto her porch. "How can I say no?"

"Simple. N-O," he said.

"You know it's not that easy," Brenna said. "I know Chief Barker is a good man, but I also know what it's like to be wrongly accused of a crime. The police miss things

88

sometimes, and they make mistakes."

"Brenna, you have to let go of what happened to you in Boston."

"That's easier said than done."

She turned to face him. He wasn't frowning anymore. He was looking concerned. It gave Brenna a case of the guilts, and she decided having him annoyed with her was infinitely more appealing than having him feel sorry for her.

"Listen, everyone has a past," he said. "But it is the past, and you can't let it dictate the rest of your life."

"Really?" Brenna asked. "Because yours certainly dictates your life by the simple fact that you never talk about it. Other than your public life as an artist, before you retired, I don't know anything about you."

"Sure you do," he said. But he looked defensive, and Brenna knew she had struck a nerve.

"I know you like baseball, you have a sweet tooth, and you love your dog. I know you were once a world-renowned artist, who got tired of the art scene and retired here. That's all I know about you. I don't know where you grew up, what kind of kid you were, or if you've ever been in love. I don't even know why you quit being an artist."

"None of that's relevant to who I am

now," he said.

"Yes, it is, because it makes you who you are," Brenna said. "You know everything about me. You know I grew up in Boston; you know I went to Boston University with Tenley; you know I was working at an art gallery when it was robbed. You even know that I was framed for the burglary and suffered a mild case of agoraphobia because of it."

Nate opened his mouth to speak, but she held up her hand, stopping him.

"Don't tell me the past doesn't dictate the choices we make," she said. "I can't let go of what happened to me in that burglary in Boston just because it's in the past. It changed who I am. It made me more cautious and careful, but it also taught me to look beneath the surface of things. People and situations are not always what they appear to be at first glance."

"Solving every crime that comes along in Morse Point won't change the way that burglary went down," Nate said. "You can't change the past."

"I know that," Brenna said. "But you can learn from it. In the past two years, Morse Point has become my home, and I like it here. I don't want to feel like I'm not safe here, and if it helps me to feel more secure by asking questions and helping to solve a crime, well, then I'm in."

"You could be putting yourself in harm's way," Nate said. He leaned against the porch rail while she fished her keys out of her bag. "I don't like that."

Brenna turned to face him. It was on the tip of her tongue to ask him why. Was he worried because he cared about her in a romantic sense? Or was he worried that he'd have to find another tenant if she managed to get herself killed?

"Nate!" a voice called from the cabin beyond Brenna's.

They glanced over to see Siobhan standing on her porch and waving at Nate. She had changed since their hike this morning and looked adorable in a denim skirt and curve-hugging sweater paired with knee-high brown leather boots.

He smiled and waved in return. Brenna had to squelch the urge to kick him.

"I'd better go see what she wants," he said.

Brenna wondered if it was just her or did he seem overly eager to go visit the new tenant? Either way, she did not like the green-eyed monster that was gnawing at her insides like Hank ripping the stuffing out of a chew toy.

"Yeah, you'd better go," she said. "You

might want to line yourself up a new dog sitter if I get myself killed."

Nate was about to step off the porch, but instead turned back to her with one eyebrow raised higher than the other. His steely gray gaze would not allow her to squirm away, even though she wanted to kick herself for sounding like such a petulant brat.

"Is that what you think?" he asked. "That I only consider you my own personal dog sitter?"

Brenna had the grace to flush as she looked down to examine the toes of her shoes. "Well, I . . ."

Her voice trailed off. The truth was that she had no idea how Nate felt about her and no idea how to tell him that.

"This probably isn't the best time for this conversation," he said. As if to prove his point, Siobhan hollered again from her porch, "Nate!"

"Probably not," Brenna agreed.

"But we do need to have a conversation," he said. "There's more between us than our mutual love for Hank and baseball."

"And baked goods," Brenna added.

He gave her a slow smile. "That, too."

He turned to step off her porch but then abruptly spun back around.

"To answer your questions, I grew up in a

small town in northwest Newyorkachusetts, which means Connecticut. I went to the Art Institute of Chicago, where I studied traditional art. And yes, I have fallen in love."

Brenna felt her heart plummet into her stomach. Was she imagining it or had his gaze intensified on that last sentence? She swallowed hard.

"So, I'll see you later?" he asked.

"Sounds like a plan," she agreed. She noticed her voice sounded hoarse, and she cleared her throat.

"And we can talk about you investigating this murder, too."

"Buzz kill," she said.

He grinned at her before he headed down the steps, and Brenna felt her insides do cartwheels. Oh, wow.

CHAPTER 8

Brenna rifled through her wardrobe looking for an appropriate outfit for a "conversation." Perhaps she should have nailed Nate down on a specific time that they would be having this conversation, but it never hurt to be prepared.

She was torn between her heather green turtleneck sweater, which made her hazel eyes appear green and made her body seem curvier than it actually was, or her chocolate brown cardigan over a matching brown shell, which made her auburn hair seem redder. Decisions, decisions.

She had turned her cell phone back on, and sure enough there were three messages from Dom. After her talk with Nate, she felt doubly guilty for hanging up on Dom. Although she had always been honest with him, and he knew she had feelings for Nate.

She decided to call him back, but before she could start dialing, a call from Tenley came through.

"Hello," she answered.

"Brenna, can you meet me at the shop?" Tenley asked. She sounded breathless, as if she'd been running.

"Now?"

"Yes, I have a lead. We must discuss."

"I'm on my way," Brenna said.

She dropped both sweaters, grabbed her purse and jacket, and dashed out the door. It was fully dark now, and Brenna flicked on her porch light and locked the door behind her.

"Brenna!" It was Nate coming back to her house.

"Oh, I'm sorry," she called over her shoulder as she ran. "I have to go."

"But . . ."

"I'll call you," she shouted.

She waved over her shoulder as she hurried to her Jeep. Nate would understand, she hoped.

But even if he didn't, she had no choice. When Brenna's life had unraveled (she was accused of a crime she didn't commit, was dumped by her boyfriend, and became afraid of her own shadow), it was Tenley who threw her a lifeline by offering her a job and encouraging her to move to Morse Point. Brenna was pretty sure it had saved her life, and in return, if Tenley asked Brenna for a kidney, it was hers. Luckily, she was only asking for help in finding a murderer.

The center of town was shut down for the evening. Only the Fife and Drum, the movie theater, and Stan's Diner were still open. Brenna parked in the alley behind the shop and came in through the back door.

She found Tenley pacing around the darkened shop.

Brenna paused in the doorway to study her friend. Her long blond hair was clipped at the nape of her neck, but stray wisps had escaped, giving her that caught-in-a-windstorm look. Her forehead was puckered in a frown, as if she were trying to remember something important but it was eluding her.

"Hey," Brenna said softly from the doorway. She didn't want to startle her.

"Thanks for coming," Tenley said. She crossed the room with her arms wide and hugged Brenna close, as if trying to draw in some of her strength.

"Anytime," Brenna said. "So, what's the lead?"

"Well, I'm still working it out," Tenley said.

"Explain." Brenna unzipped her jacket and hung it on the back of a chair, which she pulled out to sit on.

"While I was at the police station check-ing on my father, one of Uncle Harvey's girls came in."

"He had daughters?" Brenna asked.

"Four," Tenley said. She took the seat op-posite Brenna. "Just like us. I think that's one of the reasons my dad and Uncle Har-vey were so successful. They both had high-maintenance wives and several daughters."

She gave Brenna a wry smile, and Brenna knew it went without saying that most of the daughters were high-maintenance, too.

"Anyway, Kristin said something that bothered me," Tenley said. "When I told her how sorry I was, she looked so sad, but then she said, 'At least we won't have to be embarrassed by his midlife crisis anymore.' "

Brenna raised her eyebrows. "Interesting."

"I thought so," Tenley said. "You know I haven't been welcomed much into the Morse family fold over the past two years, but even I noticed that my parents and the Lesters were spending less and less time together. I mean, we used to go on vaca-tions, have barbecues, and our parents were always at the country club together."

"Why do you suppose that changed?" Brenna asked.

"I don't know, but I'm beginning to have

my suspicions," Tenley said. "You know how my father is."

"Jolly, carefree, a real card," Brenna said.

A smile flashed across Tenley's features, breaking the tension that had been evident in the tight lines around her mouth.

"Yeah," she said. "Try stern, judgmental, and inflexible."

"Silly me," Brenna said. "I must have had him mixed up with Jay Leno."

"It's the chin," Tenley said. "Happens all the time."

It was Brenna's turn to laugh.

"So, what's your theory?" Brenna asked.

"What if Uncle Harvey was having a midlife crisis, of which my father didn't approve?"

"So he shot him?" Brenna asked, horrified.

"No, no, I don't think my father is the killer," Tenley said. "He could never harm anyone, but he is a big shunner."

"Ah, yes, the highly favored method of punishment among the privileged: the shunning," Brenna said. Her own parents were big on shunning, so she could relate.

"That would explain why there seemed to be a rift between them," Tenley said. "It would also explain why Uncle Harvey wanted out of the business."

"But the question remains: who shot him?"

"I think we need to find out more about his supposed crisis."

"I'm in," Brenna said.

"Thanks," Tenley said. "I knew I could count on you."

"We need a plan."

"I already have an idea of where to start," Tenley said. "That's why I wanted to talk to you. I need a wingman."

"I'm listening."

"Have you ever been to the Morse Point Country Club?"

"No, I can't say that I have."

"Well, brace yourself," Tenley said. "Tomorrow night is ladies' night and we're going."

"Can I get in?" Brenna asked.

"I'm a lifetime member, and you're my guest," Tenley said. "No sweat."

Brenna thought about Nate and how they wouldn't be having their talk anytime soon. A tiny sigh escaped her, but she curved her lips into a smile for Tenley's sake. She'd been waiting for Nate to notice her for two years; surely she could wait another two days.

Brenna was standing in line at Stan's Diner,

waiting to see what creation he made out of her latte today. A few days ago, he had shaped her froth into a star dusted with nutmeg — a work of art, truly.

She was so busy watching Stan that it took her a moment to notice that someone was standing behind her. This would not be a problem if the person were outside of her personal space bubble. But given that she could feel hot breath on the back of her neck, the person was clearly not respecting the two-foot boundary she liked to maintain.

She turned to find Ed Johnson, looking more like a plucked chicken than ever, holding a small recorder, which he promptly shoved in her face.

"Ms. Brenna Miller, I have a few questions for you," he said.

"Not now, Ed." Brenna made her voice as chilly as an icicle on an eave — and just as pointy.

"Aw, come on," he whined. "It's just a few questions. Preston won't let me near his inn or any of his leaf peepers, and the Morse family set their dog on me. I need a quote."

"Why me?" she asked.

"Because you found the body," he said. "That's news."

Stan placed Brenna's to-go cup on the

counter in front of her. She glanced at it and saw that the froth was shaped into a chicken leg. She looked up at him, and the former navy sailor winked at her. So, she wasn't the only one who thought Ed resembled a naked fowl.

She paid for her coffee and left a hefty tip for the genius that was Stan.

"All right, Ed; one question," she said.

"Just one?" he asked.

"Yep, and there you go. That answers your question," she said. She snapped a plastic lid on her cup and headed toward the door.

"That's not fair," he protested, following her.

"Life's not fair, Ed. Harvey Lester could tell you that," she said.

"Speaking of Harvey, what was it like to find his cold, stiff corpse sealed up in a pile of leaves?"

Brenna stopped walking. The town was moving around them as if in slow motion. She could see Lillian Page emptying the book drop in front of the library. Sarah Buttercomb was drawing today's special on the whiteboard outside of her bakery. Bart Thompson, who worked at the hardware store, was helping Betty Cartwright-Hanratty load paint cans into the back of her Volvo.

She was aware of them all but not. Images of the body in the leaves came back to her in a rush, and she sucked in a breath at the gruesome impact. Someone had shot Harvey Lester, and whoever it was, was walking around among them. Brenna was sure of it.

"Frightening," she said. "It was frightening."

A flash popped, and Brenna blinked. Ed had snapped her picture while she was thinking about the murder.

"Ed!" she cried. "That was uncool."

"Oh, look at the time," he said, and glanced at his watch while shoving his digital recorder into his pocket, as if afraid she might snatch it. "Gotta go. I'm on deadline."

Brenna debated throwing her latte at him, but if she missed, she'd be even angrier that she wasted a fabulous cup of coffee on him.

She pushed open the door to Vintage Papers. Tenley was consulting with a customer who wanted to order wedding invitations. There were three other customers in the shop who were browsing, so Brenna dumped her jacket and purse in the back and came out to see if she could assist anyone.

They stayed busy up until lunch, when Tenley gratefully sank into a chair at the worktable and put her feet up.

"I didn't sleep at all last night," she said.

"I can imagine. Are we still on for to-night?"

"Yes, seven o'clock. I'll pick you up." Tenley rose abruptly to her feet and lurched toward the bathroom in the back. "I'm not feeling so well; do you mind watching the shop without me?"

"Not at all," Brenna said. "It's probably the stress; maybe you should go home for a bit and rest."

"Maybe," Tenley agreed. "But we're still going tonight."

"I'll be ready," she agreed. "Hey, what should I wear?"

"Ladies' night is really a euphemism for divorcée night, so if you want to blend, dress trampy."

"Oh, fun!" Brenna wondered if Tenley caught the sarcasm in her voice before the door shut behind her.

CHAPTER 9

Brenna was sitting on the floor doing inventory when the bells on the door alerted her that a customer had arrived. She had almost finished counting their Italian specialty papers and didn't want to have to start all over, so she called out, "I'll be right with you."

"I've heard that before," a deep voice said.

Brenna whipped her head around to find Dom leaning against the counter, watching her.

"Tunnel, huh?" he asked.

"I'm sorry. I was going to call you back," she said.

"But the tunnel collapsed and you got trapped. Then the battery on your cell phone died, and you had to dig your way out through ten feet of crumbled concrete. By the time you got out, you were suffering from dehydration and had to be rushed to the hospital, and so you couldn't return any of my calls. Don't fret, I completely under-stand. I'm just glad you're okay."

Brenna couldn't help it. She laughed. "You have quite an imagination."

"So I've been told," he said. He pushed off the counter and strode toward her, offering his hand.

Brenna took it, and he pulled her gently to her feet and gave her a solid, reassuring hug.

"I really am sorry that I didn't call you back. I got caught up talking to Tenley, and it was late before I got home. Still, it was inexcusably rude, and I'm sorry."

"All is forgiven," he said. "I really am just glad to see that you're all right."

The door jangled again, and Brenna stepped away from Dom to greet her customer. To her surprise, it was Julie with her surly son, Suede, in tow.

"Hi, Julie, Suede," she said. "It's nice to see you."

"Hi, Brenna," Julie replied. "Suede and I were just walking about town and saw the shop. I remembered you said that you worked here, and I thought we'd pop in to say hello."

"I'm so glad you did," she said. "This is my friend Dom. Dom, this is Julie. She was on the tour the other day. And this is her son, Suede."

Dom held out his hand. "A pleasure."

Julie looked a bit starstruck by him, and Brenna realized it was a reaction to the coiled energy that poured off of Dom in waves. She knew he didn't do it on purpose. Dom came from an old mob family, and Brenna was pretty sure the ability to overwhelm those around him wasn't a conscious choice but something he couldn't help because it was written into his genetic code.

Julie shook her head as if trying to break a spell, and Dom glanced at her mane of red hair as it caught the light and shimmered in a tumble of blond and copper.

They shook hands, and it seemed to Brenna that they both lingered a bit. Then Dom turned to Suede, who was giving him the curled lip of teenage surlitude.

"Suede, this is Dom Cappicola," Brenna said. She put extra emphasis on Dom's last name, and she saw Suede's eyes widen. Good, he had heard of the Cappicola family.

"Nice to meet you," Dom said. He held out his hand, and Suede reluctantly took it, but instead of your average handshake, they exchanged a flurry of backhanded slaps, curled finger handclasps, and fists pounded one atop another.

"So, how many people have you whacked?" Suede asked.

"Tommy . . . Suede!" Julie gasped in parental horror.

To Brenna's relief, Dom laughed. He had a good laugh. It rumbled up from his chest and enfolded all of them in its warmth. It made him even more charming, if that was possible.

"That's old-school," Dom said. "You know how you take care of your enemies nowadays?"

Suede shook his head. It was the first time Brenna had seen him make eye contact with any adult. He was positively entranced by Dom. Brenna couldn't blame him. That Cappicola magnetism was hard to resist. A glance at Julie and Brenna saw that she, too, was being sucked in by Dom's raw energy. The man should really come with a warning label.

"You crush them — financially," Dom said.

"But how?" the teen asked.

"You play to win," Dom said. "You make sure you are more educated and have better connections, and then you outmaneuver them in every business deal that comes your way. Pretty soon you don't need to whack them because they are no longer a threat to you or your business. This method comes with the added bonus that it's legal, and there's no body to dispose of and no jail time to serve."

"Wow," Suede breathed, impressed.

"Where did you go to school, Mr. Cappicola?" Julie asked.

"Call me Dom," he said. "I went to MIT, and you?"

"Yale."

"I thought I saw a little Bulldog in you," he said.

Julie flushed a pretty shade of pink, and Dom grinned at her. Brenna watched the exchange and felt a twinge of something unwelcome. Was it? It was — jealousy!

Mercifully, the phone rang at the counter, pulling her away from the group and this horrifying realization.

"Excuse me," she said, and she raced to the counter to pick up the phone. To her chagrin, they hardly noticed her departure.

"Vintage Papers, may I help you?" she asked.

"You have to change my order!" It was Donna Wilkins, known to Tenley and Brenna as the bridezilla from hell. She had changed her save-the-date order six times already. Both Brenna and Tenley were terrified that if she was this bad with the reminder cards for a wedding that was still a year and a half away, she would be a thousand times worse with invitations to the real deal.

"Breathe, Donna," Brenna said. "It will be all right. Let me just pull your order from the file."

She heard Donna draw a shaky breath as she flipped through the order book that they kept at the counter. She glanced over at the threesome still standing in the shop and noticed that Julie and Suede were laughing at a story of Dom's, and again Brenna felt the unwelcome surge of unhappy. What was the matter with her? Dom was just a friend. She should be happy for him if he met someone he liked. She did not feel happy, however; she felt jealous, and she didn't like it, not one little bit.

"Hello? Hello, are you listening to me?" Bridezilla was getting hysterical again.

Brenna switched her attention back to the phone. As Donna blathered on about pink versus purple embossed lettering, Brenna watched as Dom and Julie made their way to the door together, with Suede in between them like one happy little family. At the door he turned and waved.

Brenna waved back and forced a smile that felt more like a baring of her teeth.

She had to crane her neck to watch them, but sure enough the three of them headed down the sidewalk together to Stan's Diner. The phone was cordless, so she hurried across the shop to make sure, but yes, they all trooped into Stan's, with Dom holding the door for Julie and Suede.

Brenna returned to the counter, uncertain about how she felt about this sudden turn of events. She had never thought about Dom with anyone else. Obviously, he wasn't going to wait around for her forever. But she had thought . . . what? That he would wait around for her forever.

Brenna didn't like that she had taken his interest in her for granted. Feeling jealous when she saw him with Julie was no doubt just what she deserved.

With a sigh, she put the phone back in its holder. It took her a moment to realize she had hung up on Bridezilla in midsentence. Nuts!

She blew out a breath. She had better call Donna back before the girl had a nervous breakdown. Ugh.

This was not shaping up to be one of her better days.

First she had to put off Nate, now Dom was showing interest in someone else, and tonight she had to go fact gathering as a divorcée.

Brenna shook her head. They had better come up with some information tonight on who else wanted Harvey Lester dead besides Mr. Morse because if this kept up, her personal life was going to be in shambles before the killer was caught.

It took Brenna the better part of an hour to get dressed. Having never been a divorcée or attended a shindig at the Morse Point Country Club, she was flying blind, with only Tenley's suggestion to "dress trampy" to go by.

She did her best with what she had, and judging by Tenley's reaction when she saw her, she had nailed it.

"Very nice," Tenley said when Brenna answered the door at her knock. "Where did you pick that up? Hos R Us?"

"You said trampy," Brenna chided her. "Is this not the definition of working it?"

Tenley examined Brenna's tiger-print micromini, black stilettos, and clingy black top. "Your mother would have a stroke. Hey, wasn't that skirt part of your Halloween costume last year?"

"Yep, nice to get another wear out of it. Now let's see what you're wearing."

Tenley shed her coat and performed a slow spin.

Brenna laughed and said, "And you said *I* look like a ho? What is that?"

Tenley was wearing a black curve-hugging skirt that sported a thigh-baring slit, black open-toed heels, and a red silk blouse that seemed to be missing a back. She grinned at Brenna. "I think we'll do."

There was a knock at the door, and Tenley quickly snatched up her long coat. Brenna pulled on hers, too. Whoever was at the door wouldn't linger if they thought they were on their way out. Brenna opened the door to find Nate and Hank.

"Hi," he said.

"Hi back," she answered, and reached down to scratch Hank's ears.

"We were just going to take an evening walk around the lake and wondered if you wanted to join us."

"Hi, Nate," Tenley said as she moved to stand beside Brenna.

"Oh, hi." Nate glanced at their coats. "Are you two going out?"

"For dinner," Brenna said.

"To a movie," Tenley said at the same time.

Nate's gray gaze glanced between them, and Brenna got the feeling he knew they were up to something.

"Dinner and a movie," she said.

"Nate, you're just the person I was looking for." Siobhan walked up onto Brenna's porch and looped a hand around Nate's arm. "I need a big strong man to help me move some furniture. How about it?"

He smiled down at her, and Brenna had to tamp down the urge to push the other woman off of her porch.

"Sure," he said. He looked at Brenna reproachfully. "I don't have any other plans."

"Great," Siobhan said. She flipped her short brown bob in what Brenna was sure was a practiced maneuver. "See you in five."

She turned and left without ever having acknowledged either Brenna or Tenley.

"I'm going to grab our purses," Tenley said to Brenna, and she ducked back into the cabin. "Good to see you, Nate."

"You, too," he said. His gaze returned to Brenna, and she was aware that Hank sat beside them, wagging as if he were waiting for something.

She wasn't sure what possessed her to do it, but she didn't want to let Nate go to Siobhan's without giving him something to think about. She casually let go of the lapels of her coat, letting it swing open.

"So, I'll see you later?" she asked.

His only response was a nod as his gaze took in her outfit and his mouth fell slightly open, as if he'd been rendered mute.

Tenley joined them on the porch, and after locking the door behind her, she handed Brenna her purse. "Ready?"

"Yep," Brenna said. She waved at Nate as she walked passed him. He gave her a distracted wave back, and Brenna buttoned her coat, feeling pretty confident that her mission had been accomplished.

They picked their way across the lawn, trying not to let their heels sink into the ground. Tenley was driving because she knew the way, and Brenna got into the passenger seat of her friend's black sedan. She refused to look back at her cabin to see if Nate was still there.

But as Tenley headed down the drive, she couldn't resist. She gave a quick glance in the side mirror, and sure enough, Nate was still on her porch, still looking thunderstruck. Brenna smiled.

"He's so into you," Tenley said. "It's obvious in the way he looks at you."

"Interested is one thing," she said. "Doing something about your interest is another."

"True. Maybe you should wear that outfit more often around your house," Tenley said.

"He seemed quite taken with it."

Brenna tugged at the micromini that seemed determined to ride right up her back. "I don't know. This isn't exactly built for comfort."

"Fashion never is," Tenley said.

"So, what's our plan?"

"I want to mingle and see what people are saying about Uncle Harvey and my father," Tenley said. "Also, Harvey's wife, Lydia, is a fixture at the club. I'm hoping we can get some information out of her."

"Do you really think she'll be there the day after her husband was found shot dead in the woods?"

"Oh, yeah."

"I don't see anyone saying much to you," Brenna said.

"No, they'll just whisper as I pass by, but they'll try to get information out of you," she said. "Which is one of the many reasons why I am bringing you."

"What should I say if they ask about your father?" Brenna asked.

"Be vague," Tenley said. "Very vague."

"Got it," Brenna said.

Tenley turned onto the winding drive that led to the club. It was dark, but Brenna could still see the sculpted hills of the golf course to the left and the thick woods to the right.

The parking lot was near full, but Tenley pulled up to the valet station. The attendants opened their doors and traded Tenley her keys for a receipt. Tenley huffed out a breath as they climbed the sweeping stone staircase that led to the lobby.

Brenna studied her friend. "Are you all right? You look pale. We don't have to do this, you know."

"Yes, I do," said Tenley. "I know what people are saying, but my father would never harm anyone. He may not be the warmest person, but he is the pinnacle of right and wrong. I know he didn't kill Uncle Harvey."

Brenna could hear the tension and worry in Tenley's voice. She looped her arm through her friend's as they approached the coat check.

"It's going to be all right," she said. They shrugged off their coats and handed them to the girl who manned the big closet.

LADIES' NIGHT was posted on the event board, and Tenley led them down a hallway that opened up into a bar. The lights were low, the music was loud, and the place was packed. Brenna wasn't sure what she had expected, but this wasn't it. At a glance, it appeared that everyone was having a good time.

Upon closer inspection, there was a sense of desperation in the room fueled by alcohol and too much cologne. Brenna noticed that the men sipped highballs and circled the dance floor while the women danced in groups in the center of the dance floor, gyrating and grooving to the beat.

To Brenna it was like watching an episode of *Mutual of Omaha's Wild Kingdom,* where the lions were hunting the hapless antelope. The only thing missing was Marlin Perkins's voice-over.

A sweaty man in a wrinkled suit and a stringy comb-over greeted them with a leer and a wink. Ew.

"Can I buy you lovelies a drink?" he asked.

Brenna looked to Tenley for guidance. Was this guy someone that they wanted to grill for information or no?

Tenley gave a slight shake of her head, and Brenna sighed with relief.

"Thanks, but we're meeting someone," she said.

"The hot ones are always taken," he said sorrowfully. "Hey, if he doesn't show, come find me."

He gave them another wink, and Brenna had a feeling she was going to have to shower the sleazy feel of this place off of her when she got home.

"Okay." Tenley linked arms with her, and Brenna wondered if it was a self-defense ploy. "We're mingling. Keep walking. Let's check out the bar. Bingo."

Tenley turned her back to the bar and faced Brenna.

"Do you see the redhead at the bar with the martini in front of her?" she asked.

Brenna glanced over her shoulder at the bar: old guy, sweaty guy, older guy, icky comb-over guy, redheaded woman. "Yep, got her."

"That is Lydia, Harvey's wife — er, widow," Tenley said. "She knows me, but she doesn't know you. Cozy up to her and see what you can find out. I'll work the room."

"On it," Brenna said. She strode toward the bar and wiggled her way in between the icky guy and the redhead.

While the icky guy looked her over, the redhead ignored her.

She glanced at what the woman was drinking. It looked like a dirty martini, loaded with olives. When the bartender asked what she would like, Brenna said, "I'll have what she's having."

At this the redhead turned to look at her.

"Little young to be trawling for geezers, aren't you?"

Brenna looked at the woman's heavily made-up face. The cosmetics did nothing to hide the lines that were etched into the corners of her eyes and around her lips. The skin beneath her jaw was beginning to sag, and her red hair was giving way to a field of gray roots. She was leaning against the bar, as if she needed it to support her, and Brenna was guessing that this was not her first martini of the evening.

"You take 'em where you can get 'em," Brenna said.

The woman seemed to accept that with a droopy nod.

"I'm Brenna," she said.

"Lydia," the woman replied. "I'd say it's a pleasure to meet you, but I'm not planning on remembering it tomorrow."

Brenna smiled. There was something absurdly likable about Lydia Lester.

The bartender returned with her drink, and she held it up toward Lydia. "What should we drink to?"

Lydia's eyes sparkled. "Now you're talking. What to drink to indeed. How about to freedom?"

"Freedom," Brenna said. They clinked glasses, and she took a sip and felt the martini burn a trail down her throat.

"Your turn," Lydia said.

"Oh, um, how about to getting what you want?"

"Good one. To getting what you want," Lydia repeated, and clinked her glass against Brenna's. She took a healthy swallow while Brenna sipped.

Lydia was looking quite animated now. "I've had a hell of a day."

"Really?"

"Yep," she said. "I spent most of it at the police station."

She paused to take another swallow, and Brenna waited, not wanting to interrupt her.

"My husband is dead," she said.

"I'm so sorry," Brenna said.

"Don't be," Lydia said. She lifted her glass. "He was a lying, cheating, no-good rat bastard. He was going to ditch me for a younger woman. Can you believe that?"

"No," Brenna said. She really couldn't. Lydia was a character. She couldn't imagine why a man would leave her.

"To Harvey, the dumbass," Lydia said.

"To Harvey," Brenna said. They clinked and drank.

"Are you married?" Lydia asked.

"No," Brenna said.

"Stay that way," Lydia said. She raised her

glass again, and Brenna blew out a breath. Her ears were beginning to ring, but she didn't want to leave when it looked like Lydia was opening up. "To never marrying for my new friend — I'm sorry; what's your name?"

"Brenna."

"To Brenna never marrying."

They clinked and drank again. Lydia's glass was dry, so she ordered them another round. Brenna ate her olives in the hope that they would absorb some of the alcohol. As if sensing her dilemma, the bartender put a bowl of pretzels right in front of her. Brenna grabbed a fistful.

When the fresh drinks arrived, Lydia lifted her glass while swaying on her seat. Brenna reached over and righted her before she fell.

"Thank you, dear," Lydia said. "Shall we continue?"

"Oh, boy," Brenna muttered. She was not one for more than a few glasses of wine, and this martini was beginning to make her feel rubber-legged and more than a little happy. She hoped Tenley was having as good a time as she was.

She and Lydia drank several more toasts, mostly to anti-men sentiments, which could be why the icky man next to her left and Brenna was free to take his stool. When their glasses were near empty again, Lydia spun around on her stool and clapped a hand to her forehead.

"How could I have forgotten?" she asked. "We need to make one more toast."

"Really?" Brenna asked. She was now in full wobble mode and feared that standing up was going to be next to impossible.

"Yes!" Lydia cried and raised her glass. "We need to toast the man who has set me free. Here's to Rupert Morse, thanks for shooting my cheating rat-bastard husband. I owe you one."

Lydia went to take a sip but ended up falling off of her stool. Before her fanny hit the floor, however, a man in a superbly cut suit caught her under the arms and hoisted her back up. Brenna glanced up to find herself staring into the warm, dark brown eyes of Dom Cappicola.

"Well, gorgeous, we meet again," he said.

He propped Lydia onto her stool, and she tipped her head back to get a good look at him.

"Hey there, handsome," she said. "When did you get here?"

CHAPTER 10

"Mother!" A young woman came striding across the floor, looking furious. She had the same red hair as Lydia, but hers was not covering up any gray. She had large blue eyes and pale skin dusted with freckles.

She looked like the sort who could tell a good joke and liked to laugh, but not right now. At the moment she had a scowl marring her features, which made her look like she wanted to kick somebody's patoot. Brenna scooted to the far edge of her stool lest it be hers.

"With all that has happened during the past two days, you're here?" she continued her tirade.

Lydia looked at her with her eyelids at half-mast.

"Brenna, this is my daughter Kristin. Ignore her." Her voice was gin soaked and slurred. "Now back to you, handsome. Where have you been all my life?"

"Mother, control yourself," Kristin snapped. She snatched the drink from her mother's hand and shoved the glass away. "Come on, you're going home to sleep it off."

"Such a party pooper." Lydia frowned.

Kristin hauled her mother off of her stool and half carried, half dragged her to the door. The crowd parted for them, and Brenna could hear the hiss of whispers follow in their wake.

"What brings you here?" Brenna asked Dom. She tried to ignore the little flicker of hope inside of her that he had come here for her.

He smiled at her, and she could feel the energy coming off of him in waves. There was not a woman in the room who was not aware of his presence. If this really were a nature show about a pride of lions, he would unquestionably be the leader.

"I was invited by Mr. Montgomery," he said. "He's recruiting me for membership."

"Really? I don't think you fit the profile."

"Why? Because my family is formerly mobbed up?" he asked.

"No, because you still have all of your hair," she said. She gestured toward the balding, potbellied men surrounding the dance floor.

Dom flashed her a grin, and a deep laugh rumbled from his chest.

"So, did you have a nice afternoon with Julie and Suede?"

"Very nice," he said. "You know redheads are my weakness."

"Even when they come with surly adolescents?" she asked.

She tried to keep her voice neutral, but she suspected there was a tiny sprinkle of that earlier jealousy flavoring her words because Dom gave her a quick look of surprise.

"He's got some issues," Dom agreed. "But I think he's a good kid. He's just a little angry with his parents right now."

"Hmm." She went for the no-comment murmur. She really wanted to know if he was planning to see Julie again, but she couldn't figure out how to ask without sounding like she was fishing, which she was.

"So, what's with the outfit?" he asked.

"Oh, this old thing," she said. "It's nothing."

"Nothing to it, at any rate," he said. "What are you up to?"

"Me?" Brenna widened her eyes. "I'm just having drinks with friends." She glanced at his watch. "Wow, would you look at the time. I'd better get going."

She stood and feigned a big yawn.

"Yeah, I imagine butting into an investigation can be very wearying," he said.

"I'm not butting in," she protested. "If you'll excuse me, I need to go find Tenley."

"She already left," he said. "She wasn't feeling very well, and Matt arrived to take her home. She gave me her keys to give to you, but I don't think so."

"What do you mean you don't think so?" Brenna said.

"How many of those martinis did you have?" he asked.

"One — no, two. I think it was just two," she said. Her head felt fuzzy when she tried to remember.

"Yeah, I'll be driving you home," he said. "You and Tenley can come back and get her car tomorrow."

Brenna blinked at him. He was doing that mafioso power thing on her. She knew he couldn't help it, that it was as much a part of his genetic makeup as his dark hair and eyes. Still, she didn't want to seem like a complete pushover.

"Well, I suppose that would be all right," she said.

She pushed off the bar and went to walk, but her heels seemed suddenly wobbly.

Dom steadied her with a hand on her elbow. Heads swiveled to watch them go, and Dom put an arm around her waist and pulled her close, as if to protect her from the leers that followed them to the door.

"When I get you home, I am burning that skirt," he said.

"What? You don't like it?" she asked. "Tenley said I needed to look like a desperate divorcée, and this was all I had."

"There is nothing desperate about you," Dom said as he retrieved her coat from the coat check girl and helped her into it.

They walked outside into the crisp autumn air. It felt good after the sweaty bar, and Brenna inhaled deeply, trying to clear her head.

When the valet brought it around, Dom helped her into his black Volvo station wagon. He had taken her out in it once before on their only official date. Again, she marveled at the man. From a mob family, and yet he went to MIT and drove a car for its safety rating.

"So, how goes the investigation?" he asked as they headed down the drive toward the main road. "And don't bother telling me that you're not investigating Lester's murder; I know you too well."

"Lydia Lester was not exactly drowning

her sorrows in her martinis tonight," Brenna said. "We toasted freedom, and she even toasted Tenley's father for shooting her cheating rat-bastard husband."

"Not exactly grief struck," Dom agreed.

"No, but I like her," Brenna said. "She has spunk."

"Even if she's a killer?" he asked.

"It does sound as if she has an excellent motive," Brenna sighed. "But I hate to think it."

They were silent as Dom navigated the dark roads. In minutes, he was driving up the winding road to the cabins.

He parked next to Brenna's Jeep and circled the car to get the door for her. The martinis and the incredibly long day were catching up to her, and Brenna was grateful for the assistance.

He tucked her hand around his elbow and led her across the lawn to her cabin. Halfway there, her right heel sank into the grass, and her spiky stiletto was left behind. She tripped and fell against Dom, who caught her effortlessly.

They were face-to-face, and Brenna was struck again by the warmth of his gaze and the kindness of his smile. When he moved in to kiss her, she didn't stop him.

His lips were warm against hers compared

to the cool evening air, and his mouth sent a sizzle of heat spiking through her, heating her up from the inside out. The energy that always seemed to snap around him enveloped her in its embrace until she feared she might be consumed by it. She pulled back and took a shaky breath.

"I lost my shoe." She gestured behind them.

She hopped on her other foot, as if she was about to go get it, but Dom stopped her.

"Allow me," he said. He found her shoe and knelt in the grass and gently slipped it back onto her foot. She could feel the warmth of his fingers against her skin, and she shivered.

"Thanks," she said. Her voice came out breathier than she'd intended, and he smiled at her. She suspected that he knew she was not completely immune to him and was pleased.

At her door, she fished out her keys, and he unlocked the door for her. She flipped on the light and winced against the sudden brightness. The martinis were not leaving her system graciously.

"You're going to have a headache tomorrow," he said. "Do you have any pain reliever?"

"In the medicine cabinet," she said.

"Sit," he ordered. He went to the kitchen and poured her a glass of water; then he disappeared into the bathroom and came back with two over-the-counter pain tablets. "Take these and drink all of the water."

"You're pretty bossy," she said.

"Someone has to look out for you."

"I thought that was my job," a voice said from the door.

Brenna swung around to find Nate standing in the open doorway, looking none too pleased. Hank was beside him, and at the sight of Dom, he raced across the room and launched himself. Dom caught his front paws on his hip and ruffled his ears.

"How ya doing, boy?" he said. "Remember me?"

They had met once before, and given that Hank had never met a person he didn't love, it was not a big surprise that he had taken to Dom immediately. Although, Brenna had to admit, it spoke well of Dom that he seemed to like Hank just as much in return.

Brenna popped the pills into her mouth and washed them down with several swallows of water.

"I can look after myself," she said. "Thank you both very much."

"Really?" they said together, and then

exchanged a look.

Brenna narrowed her eyes. She knew that look. It was a patronizing look, as if they were commiserating on just how exasperating they found her. Well, she was not amused.

She rose from her stool and looped one hand around Dom's arm and led him toward the door.

"Thanks so much for the ride home," she said. "I really appreciate it."

She kissed his cheek. He smiled. Nate scowled.

She looped her other hand through Nate's arm and said, "And thanks so much for stopping by with Hank. I'd love to have him sleep over." And she kissed his cheek, too.

Then she gave them both a gentle shove out the door. They turned to gape at her, and Brenna gave them a tiny finger wave, just before she shut and locked the door.

Hank barked his approval, and she laughed. "Come on, Hank, let's go to bed."

He ran a loop around the tiny cabin and then did a flying leap onto her bed. By the time Brenna had finished putting on her pajamas and brushing her teeth, he was sound asleep, with his feet up in the air and his head on the extra pillow. Brenna climbed in beside him, grateful for the company.

As she was falling asleep, she thought about her evening and realized that tomorrow she and Tenley had a new mission. If Lydia was right and Harvey had been cheating, then the next step was to find out with whom he'd been playing house. Surely that person would know what Harvey had been planning, and that might lead them to the killer, assuming that his playmate wasn't the killer.

Chapter 11

"So, what did you learn from Lydia last night?" Tenley asked.

Matt had dropped her off at Brenna's bright and early, and they were driving back to the country club in Brenna's Jeep to retrieve Tenley's car.

"That dirty martinis are not my friends," Brenna said.

"So, Dom gave you a ride home?" Tenley asked. She looked like she wanted to giggle but thought better of it. "I should have warned you about Lydia and her toasts. Sorry about that."

"It's all right. I got to know her pretty well," Brenna said. "She's a little bitter about Harvey leaving her for a younger woman. She even toasted your dad for shooting the rat bastard."

"So, she thinks my father did it?" Tenley looked disturbed.

"Or she's making a lot of noise to support

that idea for reasons of her own," Brenna said.

"Do you think she did it?" Tenley asked.

"I didn't get murderess off of her," Brenna said. "But as you know, murderers don't exactly wear signs, do they?"

Tenley nodded.

"How about you? Anything interesting turn up?"

"No," Tenley said. "No one really talked to me, and I started to feel pretty lousy. Sorry I ditched on you, but once I saw Dom there, I knew you'd be in good hands."

Brenna felt her face grow warm. She was so not talking about her confused feelings for Dom right now.

"We need to find out who Harvey was shacking up with," Brenna said.

"But how?" Tenley asked. "Unless . . ."

"Go on," Brenna prompted her. "Unless what?"

"I could ask Kristin," Tenley said. "Remember she said something about Harvey's embarrassing midlife crisis. Maybe she knows who the other woman is."

Brenna remembered the very angry red-headed woman who dragged Lydia out of the bar the night before. She couldn't help but be relieved that Tenley was going to be the one to question her. Quite frankly, she scared Brenna.

After picking up Tenley's car, they both went into town to open up the shop. They did a brisk business to tourists in the morning, and lunch passed in a blur. Before Brenna knew it, it was time for her afternoon class.

"Any idea who might show up for the class today?" Tenley asked.

"None," Brenna said. "Preston offered the class to his leaf peepers as part of the nature hike, but after that trauma, I don't know how many of them have stayed in town or whether they have any interest in decoupage."

The bells on the door jangled and in walked Jan and Dan of the matching sweaters, although today it was matching sweatshirts emblazoned with DARTMOUTH across the chest.

"Hello, Brenna," Jan said. "I hope we're not late. We got distracted with today's crossword and completely lost track of the time."

"Not at all," Brenna said. "In fact, you're the first ones here. We'll be working at the table in the back of the shop. Go ahead and have a seat."

The door opened again, and this time it was Suede and Julie and the quiet blond girl, Paula. Brenna and Tenley exchanged a look. This was more than either of them had expected.

"Are Zach and Lily joining us?" Brenna asked the group.

Jan and Dan exchanged an amused look, and Jan said, "They were otherwise occupied."

It took Brenna a second to get it. "Oh. Oh!"

"Exactly," Dan said, and Jan laughed and slapped him on the arm.

"Well, let's go ahead and get started," Brenna said.

The door pushed open again, and Brenna was surprised to see Siobhan enter the shop. She sauntered to the back of the room and sat at the worktable with the others.

"Hi, Siobhan," Brenna said. "Can I help you?"

"I'm here for the class," she said. "I went on the hike, so I get to join the class. Right?"

Her voice was terse, almost challenging, and Brenna felt a hot flicker of annoyance. "Well, since two of our group can't make it, I suppose you can join in."

Siobhan gave her a smug smile, as if she'd known all along that she'd get her way. Brenna wondered if Siobhan was always this abrasive or if it was just with her. She couldn't imagine what she had done for Siobhan to dislike her so.

Brenna started opening the leaf presses she'd put on the table. As she removed each layer, she gently took out the freshly pressed leaves in rich hues of burgundy and cinnamon and gold.

"Those are lovely," Paula said.

"Thanks." Brenna smiled at her. "We're going to use them on these breakfast trays mixed in with some papers to give it a collage effect."

Brenna placed the tray she had made the week before for a different class on the table. She had painted the edges a deep chocolate brown and the bottom of the tray a mottled ecru; then she had taken an old yellowed piece of paper that she'd found in a cookbook she bought at a yard sale. It was a handwritten recipe for pumpkin bread. She glued the recipe along one side of the tray and then glued a variety of autumn leaves randomly across the tray, as if they'd been scattered by the wind. Once the glue had dried, she applied several coats of polyurethane.

"This is just one way to use the leaves on the tray," she said. "Feel free to use any papers out of our cutouts box. Tenley and I are here to assist if you need us. You should each have a tray, a glue pot and brush, a bowl of water, and a brayer. I'll be working on this tray if you want to watch and apply the same techniques to your own tray."

Brenna took an empty seat at the table and began selecting her own leaves. Suede, the sullen teenager, put his earbuds from his iPod in and promptly slumped in his chair, shoved his hands in his pockets, and ignored the group. No budding Matisse there. His mother, Julie, frowned at him but then shrugged. In the pick-your-battles game, she was obviously not engaging in this one.

Jan and Dan decided to work on one tray together. They debated the leaves and the layout, and then found a paper cutout of a male and female cardinal sitting on a nest together. They put that in the center and then worked on placing the leaves around it. Brenna was impressed, not only with how well they worked together but with how comfortable they were in their coupleness. The single girl inside of her wondered if she'd ever know that sort of connection with another person.

"I'm not sure I'm doing this right," Paula said. She was frowning at the tray in front of her. A gob of glue had puddled under one of her leaves, and it was beginning to wrinkle.

"No problem," Brenna said. "First, use a damp cloth to swab up the excess glue."

She handed Paula a rag, and the girl gently wiped up the glue around the leaf edges.

"Next, use this brayer to roll over the leaf. It'll flatten it and squeeze out more of the extra glue."

Paula did as instructed and then used the cloth to wipe up the glue again. She beamed at Brenna. "I love this."

Brenna smiled back. "I do, too."

"I don't," Siobhan snapped. "This is entirely too artsy-craftsy for me. I thought you were a real artist. This is preschool stuff."

Brenna felt her back teeth set. She was trying to like her new neighbor, really, she was, but the woman had the social skills of a stampeding rhino, and Brenna found herself longing for a tranquilizer gun.

It was on the tip of her tongue to ask Siobhan why she came to a decoupage class if she didn't like arts and crafts, but as if Siobhan read her mind, she said, "There is nothing to do in this town."

Brenna glanced at Tenley. This was her hometown, named for her great-to-the-fifth-power grandfather, and she did not take slights to it lightly.

"I guess that depends on what sorts of things you want to do," Tenley said. Unless you knew her very well, it would be hard to detect the edge to her voice.

"What sorts of things do you do?" Siobhan asked Paula.

"I'm just here on vacation," Paula said. Her voice was soft, and Brenna felt badly for her. "I really don't have plans other than what the owners of the inn plan for us."

"Well, that won't do," Siobhan said. "We single girls should all go out."

Brenna sent Tenley a look that said, "When hell freezes over."

"There's a really hot bartender over at the Fife and Drum," Siobhan said. "Let's all go for drinks after class and see who can pick him up."

Brenna had no doubt that the hot bartender to which Siobhan referred was Tenley's boyfriend, Matt. She looked at Tenley to see if she was about to blow a fuse, but Tenley was smiling. It was a calculating smile, but it was still a smile.

"That's a great idea, Siobhan," Tenley said. "Let's go after class. That means you, Brenna, and Paula, too."

"Oh, no, I couldn't," Paula began to decline, but Siobhan wasn't taking no for an answer.

"What about you, Julie?" Brenna asked. "Care to join us?"

To Brenna's surprise, Julie blushed a bright red.

"I can't . . ." Her voice trailed off, but her son added, "She has a hot date with Dom Cappicola."

"Tommy!" Julie hissed.

"What? You do," he said. He was smirking, and Brenna noticed he didn't correct his mother's use of his given name.

"I'm sorry; I know you and he . . ." Julie's voice trailed off and she looked helplessly at Brenna.

Brenna knew she felt badly about seemingly cutting in on Brenna's territory, which was ridiculous. She and Dom weren't like that.

"Don't be silly," she said. "We're just friends. I'm sure you'll have a lovely time."

If the words were stiff, that was too bad; it was the best Brenna could do.

"It's settled, then," Siobhan said. She abandoned any pretense of working on her tray and pulled a gossip magazine out of her bright green shoulder bag. She leaned back and put her feet up on an empty chair and began to flip through the glossy photos.

"Can I come?" Suede asked. He had been

watching Tenley with a moony look on his face throughout the whole class, and Brenna knew exactly why he wanted to tag along.

"No," his mother and the rest of the women answered at the same time.

He glared and lurched to his feet. He stomped off toward the bathroom in the back room, looking more like a petulant child than the man he wished to be seen as. Brenna felt for him; adolescence was just cruel.

The class put their projects on the designated shelf at the back of the shop to dry, and all but Paula headed back to the inn. Tenley and Brenna began to clean up the mess, and Paula pitched in to help, while Siobhan continued to read her magazine.

Brenna wanted to knock her feet off the chair on which they rested, but she resisted the urge. She was sure Tenley must have some reason for agreeing to this outing, although she was mystified as to what it could be.

"I'm going to freshen up," Siobhan announced. She disappeared into the small facility at the back of the shop.

"Is it just me, or is she a tad rude?" Brenna asked.

"A tad?" Tenley asked. "I've met spitting

camels with better manners."

Paula chuckled.

"Oh, sorry," Tenley said. "I suppose it's impolite of us to talk about her just because she's out of the room."

"Ack, we're turning into the Porter sisters," Brenna joked.

"I get to be Marie," Tenley called. She turned to Paula and explained, "They're our resident gossiping spinster twins. Marie is the nice one."

"Fine, I'll be Ella," Brenna said. She did an impression of Ella's scowl and tried to imitate her thick Massachusetts accent, "John Henry thought you were me. He really loved me."

Tenley put the back of her hand over her forehead and pretended to be Marie in distress, "He was the love of my life. It's such a tragedy that we were forced apart just as the bud of our young sweet love began to blossom."

Paula was doubled up with laughter. She took a breath and gasped, "I've met them! They were at Stan's Diner. They were asking me all sorts of questions."

"About the body in the woods," Brenna guessed.

"Yes, how did you know?" Paula asked.

"Nothing happens in Morse Point that the

Porter twins don't know about or want to know about or will find out about," Tenley said.

"Well, I'm ready," Siobhan announced as she reentered the room.

"Can I just use the bathroom before we go?" Paula asked.

Siobhan let out an impatient sigh. "They have one at the Fife, you know."

"I'll be very quick," Paula promised. She gave Siobhan a nervous look as she darted to the back.

Siobhan stood by the door and tapped her foot. Her irritation was plain, and Brenna got the feeling that pulling a sliver out from under her fingernail with barbecue tongs would be more fun than the outing they were about to embark on. Oh, joy.

Paula stepped out of the bathroom as Brenna grabbed their purses. Tenley locked the door behind them as they all walked out into the chilly evening air. The Fife and Drum was the best restaurant in Morse Point. It also hosted the only bar other than the Willow House, which was on the outskirts of town.

The four women entered the dark, crowded bar and found a vacant small round table in the corner. The restaurant beyond was noisy with the buzz of conversation and the clatter of plates. The bar was less packed than usual, but there was a decent crowd of regulars.

"Oh, there he is," Siobhan said. "Yoo-hoo."

Brenna glanced up, expecting to see Siobhan waving down Matt, but no, she was waving at Curtis.

She glanced at Tenley, who had her eyebrows raised in surprise. Curtis was tall, broad-shouldered, tan, and bald.

"He looks like Mr. Clean," Paula said. Brenna and Tenley laughed while Siobhan looked annoyed.

"I think he's cute," she said.

"Puppies are cute," Paula said. "I thought you were talking about the good-looking blond guy."

"Matt?" Tenley asked. She looked pleased when she added, "He's my boyfriend."

"Of course he is," Siobhan said. Her tone was mocking, and Brenna got the distinct feeling that she was putting Tenley down.

Paula must have gotten that feeling, too, because she glanced between them as an awkward silence blanketed the table.

Thankfully, a waitress arrived to take their order.

Siobhan ordered a shot of whiskey with a beer chaser. Paula ordered a glass of wine.

Tenley ordered an iced tea, which caused Siobhan to sneer. And Brenna, whose head still hurt from her martini binge with Lydia Lester, ordered an iced tea, too.

While Siobhan sauntered over to the bar to chat up Curtis, Brenna excused herself to go to the ladies' room. She was winding her way back through the restaurant when she heard someone call her name.

Lillian Page was sitting at a table with her husband, Frank. None of their five rambunctious boys were in sight. This made Brenna just the teeniest bit nervous.

Lillian must have guessed what she was thinking because she laughed and said, "Don't worry. They're all at home, tying up the babysitter, no doubt. This is our date night."

Brenna smiled. "Good for you."

"And we have a pact — we don't talk about them over dinner . . . much," Frank said.

"Are you here with Tenley?" Lillian asked.

"Yes, she's in the bar with, well, a couple of new acquaintances."

"Men?" Lillian asked, her eyebrows shooting up over her black-framed glasses.

"You're as bad as the Porter sisters," Brenna teased. "No, no men. One is a tourist from my leaf peeper group, Paula

Marchesi, and the other is Siobhan Dwyer, my new neighbor."

She gestured through the doorway to the table where Paula was seated with Tenley. While they watched, Siobhan rejoined their table.

Lillian glanced at where she pointed and then frowned.

"What?" Brenna asked.

"Oh, nothing," she said, but her voice was hesitant.

"Out with it, Lillian," Brenna said.

"Well, I can't be sure, but the brunette in there, I've seen her before."

"That's not surprising," Brenna said. "Now that she lives here, you've probably seen her in town."

"No, that's not it," Lillian said.

"Uh-oh," Frank said.

"What?" Lillian asked.

"You've got that tone of voice," he said.

"What tone of voice?" she asked.

"The one that you use when you're about to tell me something that is going to make me unhappy, like when the boys used my drop cloths for parachutes and were jumping off the roof."

"Oh, yeah, that was a rough day," Lillian said.

"Okay, so what about my new neighbor?"

Brenna asked. She had a sick feeling that Lillian was going to tell her that she'd seen her with Nate. They were grown-ups. It was really none of Brenna's business. Yeah, right.

"Well, I was at the Willow House last week with my sister, and I could swear I saw that woman, Siobhan, having coffee with Harvey Lester."

"Are you sure?"

"Absolutely," Lillian said. "Who in Morse Point carries a handbag like that?"

Brenna's eyes strayed to Siobhan's voluminous bright green shoulder bag. It was one of a kind. Well, this changed everything.

"Maybe she's a friend of the family," Brenna said. She wondered if she looked as surprised as she felt.

She forced a smile and glanced back at Lillian and Frank. "Well, good to see you both. Enjoy your kid-free dinner."

Brenna headed back to the bar. Her brain was reeling. If Siobhan knew Harvey Lester, then why hadn't she said anything to anyone? Siobhan should have expressed shock or outrage at his murder. Brenna thought back to when they discovered the body in the woods. Siobhan hadn't gotten that close to him, so she may not have been able to recognize him under the leaves. But after she'd heard who it was, surely she would have said something to someone. Brenna wondered if she had discussed it with Nate.

She slipped back onto her stool and glanced at Siobhan. She was young and perky, with her brown curly bob framing her round face, but there was an aloofness in her eyes, and her smile never quite managed to warm her gaze. She seemed to be always assessing and analyzing. Brenna got the feeling that she missed nothing.

"What?" Siobhan asked, giving her an impatient look.

Brenna realized she had been staring. Well, what the hell? She had nothing to lose here.

"A friend of mine said she saw you having coffee with Harvey Lester last week," Brenna said.

Siobhan's eyes got wide and then narrowed. "So?"

"I wasn't aware that you knew anyone from Morse Point," Brenna said.

Paula and Tenley went still, silently watching the back and forth.

"Well, you really don't know me at all, do you?" Siobhan asked.

"Apparently not," Brenna agreed. Her own voice was taking on a glacial tone.

"Look, it's no big deal," Siobhan said. "I was at the Willow House, and he came in. I let him buy my coffee, and we got to talking. I didn't even know his name until his picture ran in the *Courier* the day after he died."

"So, you just happened to meet him," Brenna said.

"Yeah, pretty freaky, huh?" she asked.

"Yeah," Brenna agreed. Siobhan was lying. Brenna could feel it, but why? She slugged back her iced tea. She wanted to get out of here and talk to Tenley. There had to be a way to find out the real connection between Siobhan and Harvey Lester.

CHAPTER 12

"I don't believe a word that girl says," Tenley said as soon as they left Paula at the inn and Siobhan had driven off back to her cabin.

Brenna noticed that Siobhan was driving Nate's pickup truck. She was trying not to let that fact gnaw at her, but it wasn't easy. The thought that Nate and Siobhan were getting cozy really bugged her. Just like the fact that Julie and Dom were obviously getting cozy as well. Here she'd thought she had two men in her life, but now she had a feeling she was going to wake up tomorrow to none.

They walked from the inn back to Vintage Papers. Tenley wanted to make sure she'd shut off the coffeepot, and it was easier to cut through the shop to get to the alley in back where they'd parked.

Brenna unlocked the front door. The bells tied to the inside handle jangled loudly in the hushed evening. She locked the door behind them as Tenley made her way to the back.

"I'm going to use the restroom," she called.

"I'll wait for you," Brenna said.

A few months before, Brenna had literally had her knees knocked out from under her in the alley behind the shop. She still didn't like going back there alone, day or night.

She rinsed out her coffee cup from earlier, checked to see that the grounds had been dumped from the pot, which was off, and straightened the counter while she waited. The door to the bathroom opened and Tenley came out, frowning at a small decoupage box she held in her hand.

"Has it done something to offend you?" Brenna asked.

"Huh . . . What . . . Oh." Tenley sighed. "No, but I'm sure I put my emerald ring in here earlier, and now it's gone."

Brenna looked inside the box. Empty. Tenley always put her rings in that box when there was a decoupage class. It kept them from getting gunky with glue.

"Maybe it's on the shelf in there," Brenna said.

"I checked," Tenley said.

"The floor?"

"Nope."

"I'll just double-check," Brenna said.

She stepped into the small restroom. There was not much surface area to examine, as it consisted of a pedestal sink, a toilet, a towel rack, and a toilet-paper holder. Painted in soft pewter with cream accents, it was a delicate-looking room. A small mirror with a shelf was the only other thing in the room, and the box Tenley was holding always sat on the shelf.

Brenna searched the tile floor, but there was nothing. Had someone from class stolen the ring? She tried to remember who might have used the bathroom, but she was drawing a blank.

She rejoined Tenley in the back room. "Sorry, no luck."

Tenley's jaw was clamped tight. "My father gave me that ring. It was my grandmother's."

Brenna remembered the round emerald set in gold with a petite diamond on each side. It was a lovely ring, and Tenley had worn it for as long as she'd known her.

"I'm trying to remember who used the bathroom," Brenna said.

"Siobhan," Tenley snapped.

"We were waiting for her for quite a while," Brenna agreed. "Although, Paula did use the restroom, too, and during class Suede did as well."

"My gut instinct is telling me that it's Siobhan. I like Paula; she's nice. I don't see her as the type to steal, and Suede, well, what would he do with a woman's ring?"

"Hock it?" Brenna suggested, but Tenley didn't seem to hear her.

"I'm going to confront her," Tenley said. "Tomorrow morning, I'll drive out to your place, and the two of us will 'pop' in on her."

"Sounds like a plan," Brenna said. "Unless you want to go tonight."

"It's tempting," Tenley said. "But I think if we wait until tomorrow, I'll have time to calm down and we can catch her off guard."

Tenley put the little box away, and Brenna locked the back door behind them as they stepped out into the alley.

"Who does that? I mean, really, who steals a family heirloom?" Tenley asked. Brenna wasn't sure if it was a rhetorical question or not, but she answered anyway.

"Someone who has no conscience," she said.

"Exactly," Tenley said. "I don't believe that she just met Uncle Harvey, either. In fact, I'd be willing to bet that she knew him — intimately."

"You think Siobhan is the one he was going to leave Lydia for?" Brenna asked.

"It makes sense, doesn't it?" Tenley asked. "She's young, pretty, and new in town. I'll bet she even came here for him."

"But Nate said an art school buddy of his asked him to put her up," Brenna said.

"We need to find out more about her," Tenley said. "A lot more."

"Is that why you agreed to go out for drinks with her tonight?" Brenna asked. "To find out more about her?"

"Well, first I thought she was eyeing Matt, and I wanted to be sure to put a stop to that," Tenley said. She only looked a little embarrassed when she said it. "But after what Lillian said, it occurred to me that Siobhan could be the one we're looking for. But now, with my ring gone and her being the most likely person to have stolen it, I have even more reasons to go after her."

She looked hurt and angry. Brenna could understand. It wasn't just a ring that had been taken. It was a link to her grandmother, a memory, something that had so much more to it than monetary value.

"Don't worry," Brenna said as she gave her a hug. "We'll get your ring back."

Tenley arrived at Brenna's cabin bright and early the next morning. She came barreling in with a box of doughnuts and two of Stan's lattes.

Brenna finished tying back her hair and popped open the top of the box. They were coconut, her favorite. This is why everyone needed a best girlfriend. They knew exactly what you needed when you needed it.

She took out two plates, and they both sat at the breakfast bar and tucked into the box.

"So, what's the plan?" she asked.

"I need to get into her place and snoop," Tenley said.

"Okay," Brenna said. She had no idea how they were going to pull this off, but she was game to try. "What's going on with your dad?"

"He's at home," Tenley said. "The medical examiner placed Uncle Harvey's death sometime the evening before you found him. My father was at a business meeting in Boston."

"So he's clear?" Brenna asked. She bit into her doughnut and felt more at peace with the world than she had in days. Sadly, it didn't last.

"Not quite," Tenley said. "They are trying to pinpoint his traveling time. They seem to think he had time to murder Uncle Harvey after his meeting and still get home in time for a nightcap with my mother."

"What about Lydia? If Harvey was cheating on her, surely she had the most to lose if he left her."

"She was at the club all night with plenty of witnesses." Tenley was silent while she chewed, and Brenna wondered what she was thinking.

"We need to find out where Siobhan was on the evening that Harvey was murdered."

"She's been spending a lot of time with Nate," Brenna said.

"Oh."

"Yeah, I'm not sure what's going on there, but there's no time like the present to find out."

Brenna rose from her stool and closed the lid on the doughnut box. She picked up her latte and said, "Are you ready?"

"As I'll ever be." Tenley picked up her latte and followed.

As they stepped onto Brenna's front porch, she heard the front door to Siobhan's cabin open. Instinct made her stop short, and Tenley plowed into her back.

"What the . . . ?"

"Shh." Brenna pushed her back inside and then quickly shut her door. "Come on."

She hurried across her small cabin into her bedroom, which overlooked Siobhan's cabin. The morning sky was just beginning to lighten, but there was no mistaking two things. One was Siobhan in a bathrobe that looked like a hot pink kimono; the other was a tall, dark-haired man with a severe case of bed head, who had her locked against him in a passionate embrace.

Nate! Brenna felt her insides clench tight. She didn't want to believe it. She didn't want to watch, but she couldn't look away.

"Is that . . . ?" Tenley's voice trailed off.

"I think so," Brenna said. Her voice sounded weak.

"What is he doing with her?" Tenley sounded bewildered.

"I can only imagine," Brenna answered, unable to keep the sarcasm out of her voice.

"No, I don't mean that," Tenley said. "I get that. What I want to know is how those two know each other."

"He's her landlord," Brenna said.

"I thought Nate was her landlord," Tenley said.

The couple broke apart, and Brenna caught a swift glance of the man's profile. His nose was small and looked as if it struggled to keep his glasses up.

"That's not Nate," she said.

"You thought it was?" Tenley asked.

Brenna had the grace to blush. "Just for a second."

"Oh, puleeze, that man is crazy about you," Tenley said. "He'd never go for that bit of fluff."

"Then who is that guy?" Brenna asked, changing the subject.

"That is Brian Steele, the young executive my father wanted to toss me at," Tenley said.

"You never went to that dinner, did you?"

"No, Uncle Harvey's murder threw a wrench into that plan."

Siobhan suddenly glanced their way. "Get down!" Brenna hissed, yanking Tenley down out of the window. They crouched on the floor cradling their lattes.

"Now what?" Tenley asked.

"No idea," Brenna said. "I have a lot of questions and no answers."

"Let's go over to Siobhan's," Tenley said.

"Or . . ." Brenna scooted up the wall to glance back out the window.

"Or?" Tenley prodded.

"One of us could chum up to Brian and see what he can tell us."

Tenley suddenly turned pale and sweaty.

"Are you all right?" Brenna asked.

"Just a little stomach sick." Tenley swallowed convulsively.

"That bad, eh?" Brenna asked. "Well, don't worry. I wasn't thinking you should be the one to approach him. He knows you;

he doesn't know me. I'll be less suspicious."

Tenley blew out a breath and nodded. "Sounds like a plan. I don't think I can face Siobhan right now."

"Let's see what we get from Brian first," Brenna said. "Then we can go after Siobhan."

Brenna watched Tenley leave. She still looked a little pale, and Brenna was worried for her friend. This situation with her father was really stressing her out. Brenna wished she could help more, but until they had some idea of who could have shot Harvey, Tenley's father would likely stay in the hot seat.

She needed more information on Lester and Morse, Inc., and there was only one person she knew who might have that information: Dom Cappicola.

He answered on the third ring. "Hey, gorgeous."

"Hi, Dom," Brenna said. She felt her face grow warm.

"Don't tell me; let me guess," he said. "You've decided you're madly in love with me and you want to run away with me."

"Uh . . . no. Besides, I hear you have a new 'gorgeous' in your life," she said. Okay, she was prying. She knew it, but she couldn't seem to stop herself.

Dom laughed. "Oh, no, there's only one 'gorgeous' in my life. There is, however, a 'beautiful.' "

"Really," Brenna said. "Do tell."

"No can do," he said. "You aren't by any chance jealous, are you?"

"Certainly not!" Brenna insisted. She winced as soon as the words escaped, knowing that she'd said it with entirely too much force.

Sure enough, Dom chuckled. "If you say so."

"I do," she said, but she could still hear the amusement in his voice.

"So, what can I do for you this fine morning?" he asked.

"I am wondering if you've ever heard of Lester and Morse, Inc.?"

"The electronics import company? If I remember right, my father tried to buy them a few years ago."

"Really?"

"Yes, but they held him off."

"So, it was more of a takeover type of thing?"

"When my father was in charge, everything was a takeover sort of thing."

"Ah," Brenna said. "Would you have any information on them?"

"Because . . ."

Brenna grabbed her hooded sweatshirt and stepped out onto her porch. She glanced at the smooth lake and admired the way the colorful trees were reflected on its glassy surface. How much should she tell Dom? Enough for him to gather information but not so much that it would cause him problems.

She sat on one of the padded chairs that faced the water and propped her feet up on the rail.

"I am just wondering if you know anything about their current financial situation," she said.

"You want me to use my contacts to substantiate the rumors that Lester wanted out and Morse couldn't afford to buy him out so Lester was looking to sell his half to a rival company that would essentially shut them down?"

"Is that true?" Brenna asked. "How do you know these things?"

"I'm good at what I do," he said. "Besides, Lester approached me a few weeks ago. I turned him down, and last I heard he was planning on selling to a rival, who would close up Lester and Morse for good."

"You are good," Brenna said.

"Who's good?" a voice asked.

Brenna dropped her feet and spun around to see Nate stepping up onto her porch.

"Oh, hi," she said. "Be right with you."

Nate nodded and leaned against the rail, crossing his arms over his chest.

"Don't tell me; let me guess. It's *him,*" Dom said.

"Correct."

"So, are you two a thing yet?" he asked. "I figured my showing up with you the other night would motivate him to get off his butt."

"Yeah, not that I've noticed," she said.

"Does that mean I can ask you out and you'll say yes?"

"I don't know about that," she said. "Sounds as if you're busy."

"You *are* jealous. Nice. You know I can always make time for you. All you have to do is say the word," he said.

Brenna was silent, unsure of how she felt about this turn of events.

"I'll do some more digging and see what I come up with," he said.

"Thank you," Brenna said. "And if you come across the name Brian Steele, I'd be very interested to know what you find out."

"On it," he said. "See ya, gorgeous."

Brenna felt Nate watching her and was chagrined that she couldn't keep her face from turning red.

"Dom?" he asked.

"Yeah, he's looking into something for me," she said.

"The Lester murder," Nate said.

"Not exactly," she said.

"But . . ."

"He might have some information about their business for me," she said. "I'm curious to know what their financial situation is."

"Why not ask Mr. Morse?"

Brenna tried to imagine it. No, that conversation would not go well no matter how circumspect she was.

"I thought so," Nate said. He took the seat beside her. "You really need to stay out of this. Chief Barker will figure out who shot Lester."

"But it doesn't look good for Mr. Morse," Brenna said.

"If he's innocent, then he has nothing to fear," Nate said.

"But Tenley is worried, and she's asked for my help," Brenna said. "How can I refuse?"

Nate sighed.

"Can I ask you something?" she asked. "What do you know about Siobhan?"

"Not much," he said. "She's young and

cute and seems to be well educated. Why?"

"She knew Harvey Lester," Brenna said. "She was seen at the Willow House with him the week before he died."

Nate raised his eyebrows. "What does she say about that?"

"That they just met, that she didn't really know him."

"But you don't believe her."

"I don't know," she said. "It seems like quite a coincidence."

"Morse Point is a small town," Nate said. "It seems perfectly reasonable that she might have met him by chance."

"Really?" Brenna asked. He sounded like he was defending Siobhan, which she found extremely annoying.

"I think it's suspicious."

"You think everything is suspicious, and yet you're friends with a known mobster," he said.

"He's not a mobster," Brenna protested. "He's trying to turn the family business legitimate."

"So he says. I don't think you should be hanging around with him. It's just asking for trouble."

"Why are you being like this?" she asked.

"Like what?" he asked. He rolled up from his seat to stand and then began to pace.

"Argumentative — no, bossy." She stood, too.

"Maybe it's because you're so stubborn."

"I am not."

"Are you going to keep nosing around this murder?" He stopped in front of her and planted his hands on his hips.

"Yes, my friend asked for my help, and I'm going to give it to her."

"See? Stubborn," he snapped. With that, he turned on his heel and stomped off the porch. Brenna watched him stride across the lawn, still muttering to himself.

"Huh." She turned and stomped back into her cabin, slamming the door behind her so that it rattled on its hinges. She hoped he heard it.

Chapter 13

"How do you know he's going to be at the Fife and Drum at eight?" Brenna asked.

"I called my dad's secretary and had her call Brian and tell him to meet my father there."

"And she did it?"

"Of course," Tenley said. "I told her that I was calling on behalf of my father because he's so busy."

"You realize you're going to be in the soup if Brian questions your father and he questions his secretary and she tells on you."

"If my father goes to jail for a crime he didn't commit, then it's worse than the soup. The Morse family goose is cooked. This is just a little white lie."

Brenna spun away from her closet. "Okay, how do I look?"

"Fabulous," Tenley said. She looked over Brenna's gray jersey Vanessa Bruno curve-hugging, asymmetrical dress and sighed.

"You had such a fabulous wardrobe when you worked at the art gallery in Boston. Do you ever miss it?"

Brenna knelt down and straightened the lace on her black Burberry lace-up ankle boot. They were pretty and delicate, but the heel was higher than she was used to and she could feel her feet already beginning to protest.

"Honestly?" she asked. "No. I loved working with the artists and their work, but the snooty clients? Not so much. I like it here."

Tenley gave her a fierce hug. "I'm so glad."

Brenna saw the sheen of tears in Tenley's eyes.

"Hey, are you all right?" she asked.

"I'm fine." Tenley waved her hand. "Just a little overtired."

"Well, let's get this over with so you can try and get some shut-eye tonight," Brenna said. "You need your rest."

"Why? What makes you say that?" Tenley asked. Her eyes were wide, and she looked the teensiest bit paranoid.

"Because you have a business to run and you can't do it if you're falling asleep at the cash register," Brenna said. "Now, come on, let's focus."

"Oh, yes, of course, you're right," she said. "Okay, let's go over the plan in the car."

Brenna locked her cabin door behind them as they made their way to her Jeep. She couldn't help but notice that Tenley had been behaving oddly lately. They had to solve Lester's murder, and soon. If Tenley got any jumpier, she was going to give herself a heart attack.

Brenna sat at the bar, sipping the Chardonnay Matt had poured for her and trying not to look out of place. Tenley had posted herself by the door to signal when she saw Brian arriving.

At ten minutes to eight, Tenley walked over to the bar and ordered a cranberry spritzer. This was her signal that Brian was just entering the room. Then she disappeared so that he wouldn't see her.

Brenna tossed her hair over her shoulder and tried to look casual. The tall, dark-haired man she recognized as Brian sat down at the bar several stools from her, and she sighed. She had hoped he'd sit beside her to make chitchat easy, but no.

He was busy tapping on his smartphone and barely looked up from it to order a beer from Matt, so Brenna took the opportunity to study him. Matt delivered the beer and tried to engage him in conversation, but Brian merely grumbled and turned his back to him. Obviously, he was lacking in social skills, which could explain why he and Siobhan were such a good fit.

Matt came over to Brenna and rolled his eyes. "You look amazing. The man must be completely near-sighted."

"Or just uninterested," Brenna said. She took a hearty swallow from her wine. "Wish me luck. I'm going in."

She slipped off of her stool, feeling as if everyone in the bar was watching her, which was ridiculous. Most of the people were on dates or watching the sports channel on the TV behind the bar.

She strode the three stools to where Brian sat, still tapping away at his phone, and sat on the vacant seat beside him. She crossed her legs where he could see them. Nothing. She tossed her hair. Nada. She leaned provocatively against the bar. Zip. She debated smacking the phone out of his hands but thought that might be construed as rude and not get her the information she was seeking.

"Come here often?" she asked.

"Huh?"

Brenna resisted the urge to sigh. Instead, she forced herself to smile and repeat, "Do you come here often?"

"No," he said. He finally looked up, and

she got her first real look at the hotshot young exec Tenley's father had been trying to get her to date.

He was good-looking in a corporate way. The close-cropped short hair, the fitted suit, the small frameless glasses, the pasty skin from too much time spent in fluorescent lighting. Yeah, he had it going on in a buttoned-down sort of way.

Now that he was looking at her, Brenna turned up her smile and said, "I'm Lynn." She figured it wasn't really a lie if she gave him her middle name, and this way, if Siobhan had ever mentioned her name to him, he wouldn't put it together.

"Brian," he said.

"So, what do you do, Brian?" she asked.

He looked left and right, as if scouting the nearest exit. Brenna couldn't blame him. If the conversation grew any more boring, she'd be looking to escape herself. It was five minutes past eight o'clock. He was probably wondering where Mr. Morse was.

With a sigh, he answered, "I work for an electronics import company."

"That sounds fascinating," she said in what she hoped was an encouraging voice.

"No, it doesn't," he said.

Okay, so much for winning him over with

her charm. "You're right. That sounds really dull."

This got a small smile from him, and for the first time, he looked at her as if he was really seeing her.

"And what do you do that is so fascinating?" he asked.

Brenna saw Matt hovering nearby with a small smile on his lips. He would no doubt be reporting to Tenley that it was going well.

"I work in a paper store," she said.

Brian slipped his phone into his jacket pocket and took a sip of his beer. "Oh, now, *that* is intriguing."

"Are you mocking me?" she asked.

"A little," he said. "So are you in charge of the Post-its, Lynn?"

"The stationery, actually," she joked in return. "It requires advanced skills."

"In paper pushing?" he asked.

"Precisely," she said. He smiled again, and Brenna thought that she had been too harsh before. He really was quite good-looking.

"Well, since we're both in such scintillating careers and since my boss seems to be running late," he said, "would you care to order some appetizers with me? I'm starving."

"That'd be nice," she said. "Thank you."

Matt handed them menus before they

even asked.

"Great service here," Brian said.

"Indeed."

They ordered several appetizers to share, and Brian turned back to Brenna. "How long have you lived in Morse Point?"

"Just about two years," she said. "And you?"

"A few months," he said. "I work for Lester and Morse."

"Oh." Brenna opened her eyes wide, as if this were news. "Wasn't one of them found . . ." She let her voice trail off, as if she hadn't been the one to find Lester's body.

"Shot in the woods? Yes."

"Do they have any idea who might have done such a thing?" she asked.

He looked hesitant, as if he wasn't sure how much he should say.

"Well, the police are very interested in Mr. Morse," he said. "Being Lester's partner, I suppose that makes sense. They're also looking at Mrs. Lester, although I heard she has an alibi."

"Who do you think did it?" Brenna asked. She kept her gaze on his face, looking for what she didn't know, but she didn't want to miss so much as a flicker of an eyelash.

He leaned close. "Between you and me?"

"Yes, absolutely." Brenna felt her pulse pound in her ears as a rush of adrenaline coursed through her. This was it. She was going to find out something vital.

"I don't have a clue," he said. He sat back with a grin, and Brenna realized he was teasing her.

"Very funny," she said. "You got me."

Matt returned with a heaping sampler plate of appetizers, which included potato skins and mozzarella sticks as well as cut vegetables and chicken wings, and Brenna realized she was ravenous. They each dished some of the samples onto their plates.

The Fife made some of the best appetizers in town. Brenna tried to maintain a semblance of decorum, but it was not easy, as the hollowed-out potato skins were stuffed with mashed potatoes mixed with Gorgonzola, bacon, and caramelized onions. It took all of her powers of concentration not to forget to question Brian while they ate.

"If you have no idea who killed Lester, then do you think the police do?"

Brian chewed and then washed it down with a sip of beer. "Chief Barker came into the office and asked a lot of questions, but I didn't get the feeling he had the case solved. Why the interest?"

Brenna lowered her eyes to her plate and tried for nonchalance. She shrugged and said, "Just ghoulish curiosity."

Brian said nothing, and when she glanced back up, he was staring over her shoulder with an intensity that made her turn around, half expecting to find the grim reaper standing there.

But no, it was Siobhan and Nate. They had just entered the bar, and she was leaning on his arm and smiling up at him. Brenna felt a giant fist squeeze her insides.

Nate looked particularly handsome in a charcoal gray gansey, which turned his eyes a deep shade of slate, over black slacks, while Siobhan had the whole coquette thing going with a ruched crepe minidress in a bold shade of tangerine that Brenna recognized as a Stella McCartney design. She had to squelch the desire to lob a Gorgonzola potato at the girl.

As if he sensed her presence, or perhaps because he felt her laserlike stare burning a hole in his forehead, Nate glanced over at the bar and saw her sitting with Brian. His eyebrows rose in surprise. He looked as if he might come over, but Siobhan steered him to the hostess, who led them into the adjoining dining room.

Brian stared at the door they had just

walked through as if willing them to re-appear. They did not. He tossed his half-eaten potato down in disgust.

"Are you all right?"

"Yeah, I've just lost my appetite," he said. He pulled his phone out of his pocket to check the time.

"It looks like I've been stood up."

He rose from his seat and threw a wad of bills on the bar. "It was nice to meet you, Lynn."

"You, too," Brenna said, almost forgetting the fake name she'd given him.

He strode from the bar, his steps slowing for only the tiniest fraction as he passed the door to the dining room, and Brenna was sure he was looking for Siobhan.

It wasn't hard to see that Brian was in love with Siobhan. The question was how did they know each other, and how did she know Harvey Lester? And why was Nate having dinner with Siobhan?

Okay, that last one was really just for her, but still. If she was going to get any answers, her best bet had just stormed out the door. With a wave to Matt, she grabbed her purse and hustled after him.

CHAPTER 14

"Brian, wait!" Brenna called. He was rounding the corner. She had to catch him.

She poured on the speed, but she wasn't used to running in heels, and she felt a little ridiculous, not to mention nervous about tripping and falling.

Luckily, he heard her and turned around. His face had been hopeful-looking, but it shifted into a frown when he recognized Brenna. Obviously, he had been hoping it was Siobhan racing after him.

"Look, you seem very nice," he said. "But I'm really not interested."

Brenna skidded to a halt before him. She was panting and out of breath, so it took a minute for his words to sink in.

"Excuse me," she gasped.

"I think it's better for me to be straightforward, don't you?"

Brenna sucked in a lungful of the sweet evening air and nodded. She hadn't quite caught her breath yet.

"You're a lovely woman, really, but I think you're just a little bit too old for me," he said. He pushed his glasses up on his nose and gave her a sympathetic look.

"Too old for you?" Brenna spluttered. "How old do you think I am?"

Brian must have sensed danger in the air because he looked nervously from left to right, as if hoping someone would appear and save him.

"I don't really think we need to get specific, do we?" he asked. "I mean, you're a mature woman, a cougar, if you will, and I am a guy in my prime . . ."

Brenna wondered how his prime was going to hold up when she kneed it up into his throat.

"Listen, you moron," she said. "I am not interested in you in that way. What I *am* interested in is the woman who just walked into the Fife with Nate Williams."

Brian's eyes widened behind his glasses. "I don't know who you mean."

"Yes, you do," Brenna snapped. "I saw your face when she walked in there. I'm betting you know her — very well."

Brenna paused to take a deep breath. She had to play this very carefully. How could she present herself so that Brian would talk to her but not tell Siobhan? If he described her, Brenna had no doubt that Siobhan would know it was she who had been questioning Brian, and that would put Siobhan on her guard.

"You're wrong. I was thinking of something else," he said.

"Really?" Brenna asked. "Because I am interested in the man who she just walked in there with, and I want to know what their relationship is. Are they involved?"

"I can't help you," he said. He clenched his teeth, as if Brenna might try to open his mouth and pry the words loose.

"Does she always go for older men?" she asked.

Brian blinked at her, and Brenna knew she had startled him. "Has she been involved with any other older men, like your boss, Harvey Lester? I heard they were seen together."

"I don't know her," he protested, looking panicked. "I'm telling you I don't know her."

"Is she sleeping with Nate Williams?" she asked. She hoped she sounded like a jealous girlfriend, which really wasn't a stretch at the moment, to keep him from being suspicious about her questions about Lester.

"No . . . uh . . . I don't know," he said. "I

don't know her. I don't know you. Now, leave me alone. Okay?"

Before Brenna could question him further, he spun on his heel and ran away. Brenna let him go.

It was a good thing she had a healthy self-esteem, she thought, as she made her way back to Vintage Papers. Otherwise, his reaction and rejection of her might have stung.

She let herself in the front door and locked it behind her. She and Tenley had agreed to meet here to discuss what Brenna had learned from Brian. She was disappointed that she didn't have much to offer. She and Tenley were going to have to think of another way to get information on Siobhan.

Tenley was sitting at the back table with a pot of tea and a paper manufacturer's catalog. She closed the catalog and sat up as soon as Brenna sat down next to her.

"What happened?" Tenley asked. "What did you find out?"

She filled another cup of the steaming-hot nut-flavored tea and handed Brenna a spoon and the honey pot.

Brenna sighed. She hated feeling as if she'd let Tenley down. She stirred a fat dribble of honey into her tea and took a bracing sip.

"He denies knowing Siobhan at all," she said. "He basically stonewalled me and then stormed off. Of course, I couldn't very well say I'd already seen them together in front of her cabin. But the look on his face when she walked in tonight said it all. He is in love with her. Ugh, what a mess."

"Wait. Back up. She came into the Fife?"

"Yes, with Nate for dinner."

Tenley let out a loud gasp. "No!"

"Yes."

"Was it a date?"

"I don't know." Brenna sipped her tea. She knew she sounded as miserable as she felt.

"It wasn't," Tenley said, sounding definite. "The man likes you; he's always liked you. He could not possibly date *her*."

Brenna could have kissed her. But sadly, she had to face the reality that Nate was on a date with Siobhan.

"Apparently, Siobhan is the sort of woman who likes to be dating a pair and a spare at all times," Brenna said.

"What do you mean?"

"A pair, Nate and Brian, and a spare, well, that would have been Harvey. I wonder if she is trying to line up some other poor sap to take his place."

"Wow, I can barely handle one man,"

Tenley said.

"In any event, the bigger issue is that I did not get any information from Brian about Siobhan's relationship with Lester, which means we're going to have to find another avenue for information."

"I say we follow Siobhan and jump her," Tenley said. "Then we tie her up and make her talk."

"Um, not for nothing, but you have a kind of crazy glint in your eye, and it's making me nervous," Brenna said.

"Oh, sorry; I'll try to rein it in," she said. She picked up her fine china teacup and took a delicate sip.

"Right, then I think we need to figure out how to get background information on Siobhan."

"Too bad she's not from around here," Tenley said. "The Porter twins would have an entire dossier on her."

"I wonder where she *is* from," Brenna said. "There has to be a way to find out. Nate said that an artist friend of his asked him to put her up for a few weeks. But how does this artist friend know her?"

"Maybe she was dating him, too," Tenley said.

Brenna sighed. Her brain was tired of spinning in circles, and her feet were beginning to hurt. "I should just ask Nate."

"Oh, and that won't be awkward," Tenley said.

"It doesn't have to be. I mean, if nothing else, Nate and I are friends; surely I can ask him about my new neighbor and not reveal how much I'd like to choke her for going on a date with him."

Tenley cracked a smile at her. "You know the one thing I have always loved about you is your honesty."

Brenna tipped her head in acknowledgment and said, "Likewise."

There was a knock on the glass door, and they both turned to see Matt standing out front. Tenley jumped up and hurried around the table to unlock the door and let him in.

They shared a quick hug and then Tenley stepped back and snapped, "What are *you* doing here?"

Brenna glanced up at her tone and saw Nate follow Matt into the shop. She had a heart-stopping second of thinking Siobhan might be with him, but no, he was alone.

"Nice to see you, too," Nate said affably.

"Where's your date?" Tenley asked, obviously not ready to play nice just yet.

"I was not on a date," Nate said. "I was on a fact-gathering mission. Isn't that right, Matt?"

"Indeed," Matt agreed. He took Tenley's arm and led her back to where Brenna sat. Nate followed.

"Nate called me this afternoon, and we set it up. I knew you were upset about your ring and that you suspected Siobhan. I thought maybe Nate could work his artist's charm on her and get some information."

"So you're not dating her?" Brenna asked as she stood up. She needed to look into his piercing gray eyes and see the truth for herself.

"Heck no, she's a total pain in the keister," he said, looking at Brenna as though she were having a mental episode. "I only took her out to get information for you."

"You did that for me?" she asked.

"Yes, and you owe me at least two batches of brownies with the chocolate chunks in them," he said, looking disgruntled. "You know I don't like people as a rule, and making conversation with her about killed me."

"Oh, Nate," Brenna said. She was touched, truly.

"Not so fast," he said. "You have some explaining to do. Who was the guy?"

"Guy?" Brenna asked. She was still processing the fact that Nate just called Siobhan a pain. He didn't like her. He wasn't dating her. She almost broke into a Snoopy dance of joy.

"Yeah, you remember the guy at the bar," he said. "He was young, skinny, and looked like he starched his underwear. You were sharing food with him — you know, that guy."

"Brian?" she asked. "He was an idiot. I wasn't with him; I was merely trying to get information from him about Siobhan because Tenley and I saw them together this morning."

"So, you weren't on a date?" he asked.

"Oh, heck no," she said. "Why would you think that?"

"I wonder," he said. He turned and glared at Matt, who was studiously examining a new shipment of handmade papers. "Brenna Miller, I think we've been set up."

"I don't understand," she said.

"Don't you find it odd that I thought you were on a date, and you thought I was on a date?" he asked.

"Well, that's what it looked like," she said. "But it is quite a coincidence that we ended up at the Fife at the same time, isn't it?"

"Or is it?" he asked.

"I can explain," Matt said. "I kind of thought if you saw each other with someone else it might give you a kick start, so to speak."

"Matthew Collins, were you matchmaking?" Tenley asked.

"I just figured since I knew you were both going to be trying to get information from people of the opposite gender tonight . . ."

"It seemed like a good idea to make sure they ran into each other," Tenley finished.

Nate turned from them to Brenna, looking completely exasperated. "You know, even when I was world famous, I don't think I had as many people in my business as I do in this town. So, you really weren't on a date?"

"No," she said. "And you weren't, either?"

"No," he said.

"Oh, Nate." Brenna didn't stop to think. She was so relieved that he hadn't been out with Siobhan she could barely stand it. She circled the table and threw herself at him.

Nate caught her easily and hugged her close. He squeezed her hard, and when they leaned back and looked into each other's eyes, he kissed her.

The attraction that had been held in check for too long between them was now free to run wild, and it took them over and under as they kissed with a thoroughness that left them both dazed and wanting more. Brenna's vision went fuzzy, and her breath was coming fast. When she stepped back and looked at Nate, he seemed as undone as she was.

She ran a shaky hand through her hair. "Uh, yes, well . . ."

He smiled at her. "How about those Red Sox?"

She laughed, and the tension was broken. She noticed that Matt had his arms around Tenley's waist, his chin resting on her shoulder, and they were both grinning at them. Oh, whatever.

Brenna sat back down at the table. "So, what did you find out from Siobhan?"

Nate sat beside her and laced his fingers through hers. It was a gesture of intimacy that flattened her almost as much as his kiss.

"Unfortunately," he said, "not much. I wanted to ask pointed questions, but I didn't want to make her suspicious. In the end, she evaded every question by changing the subject or answering a question with a question. Very annoying."

"Is there any way to contact your artist friend and see what he knows?"

"I've already sent him an e-mail," Nate said. "He's traveling in Europe, so I don't know how long it will take him to get back to me."

"Well, since Brian lied about knowing Siobhan, and Siobhan is being very wily, I think

187

I need to go to the source. I need to ask my father just what he knows about Brian," Tenley said.

"Do you think your father knows that Brian and Siobhan are involved?" Matt asked.

"You didn't tell me that," Nate said. "Those two are a couple?"

"We think so. Tenley and I saw them together at her cabin. And as I recall, I didn't tell you because I was too busy being mad at you for telling me to mind my own business," she said.

Nate squeezed her fingers. She took it to mean he was sorry. She squeezed his fingers back, letting him know it was okay.

"Do you think your father will tell you anything?" Brenna asked Tenley.

"If I ask in the right way," she said. "Looks like I'm going to have to invite myself to Sunday dinner."

"Invite me, too," Brenna said. "I don't want you going in there alone."

"Me, too," said Matt. Tenley opened her mouth to protest, but Matt shook his head. "This is nonnegotiable. I don't want you going anywhere near your family without me there to protect my interests."

Tenley stared at him, and then she nodded. "You're right. They've been too successful at splitting us up in the past. We're not going to let them do that again."

Matt leaned over and kissed her temple. "That's my girl."

CHAPTER 15

Sunday dinner at the Morse house. Brenna knew she could have let Tenley go on her own, and now with Matt going, she wasn't sure who she was there to support more, Tenley or Matt.

Normally, she figured Matt could hold his own, but this wasn't going to be a fair fight. Matt and Tenley were going to be woefully outnumbered by her three sisters and their families and Tenley's parents. It was like sending them into an ambush. Brenna had to go and at least try to watch their backs.

Tenley was nervous all morning, so Brenna offered to drive. Matt was meeting them there. They wound their way up Laurel Hill, where all of Morse Point's larger estates resided. Brenna turned right and headed down the immaculately sculpted landscape of the Morse family residence.

Stately oaks lined each side of the gravel drive, creating a blazing canopy of branches that hung overhead.

Flower beds rich with chrysanthemums in every color skirted the hem of the enormous three-story Colonial that came into view as they left the trees and parked on the edge of the circular drive.

A slate staircase led up to a portico that was decorated with a fat bunch of cornstalks tied together and braced by a small pile of pumpkins.

The October sky was overcast, and a bitter wind tugged at their coats as they left the warmth of the car and made their way to the front door. Tenley knocked just as Matt's car, a silver sedan, parked behind Brenna's.

The door opened, and the housekeeper, Mrs. Winslow, gave Tenley a warm smile. "Miss Tenley, it is so good to see you."

"Thank you, Mrs. Winslow," Tenley said, and reached over to grasp the plump woman's hand. "This is my friend Brenna and my . . . boyfriend, Matt Collins."

Mrs. Winslow's eyebrows shot up in surprise, but she smiled at both Brenna and Matt and ushered them inside. She took their coats and told them that the rest of the family was waiting in the parlor and dinner would be served in thirty minutes.

Tenley led the way down the austere

hallway. The walls were eggshell; the floor was wooden. There were no other decorations to be seen. Brenna craned her neck to see into other rooms, but there was nary a picture nor a tchotchke to be found. If Brenna didn't know better, she'd wonder if anyone lived here.

Tenley paused in front of a set of large walnut double doors. She looked pale and a little shaky.

"Are you ready?" Matt asked. "Do you want me to go? Will this be easier for you if I'm not here?"

Tenley glanced up at him with a look of such adoration that Brenna felt as though she was intruding on something private and looked away.

"No, you're with me, and I'm proud that you're with me," Tenley said. She rose up on her tiptoes and kissed his cheek. Then she let out a sharp breath. "Ready or not, here we come."

She turned the knob and pushed the door on the right open. The first thing Brenna noticed was the large fireplace across the room, crackling and popping with a cheery fire in it. The air in the large house was cold, and she longed to go sit on the hearth until she felt as warm as a piece of toast.

The next thing she noticed were the eight

pairs of adult eyes staring at them, their gazes ranging from concern to disapproval. The children, who looked to range in age from five years old to a tiny baby, completely ignored them, which Brenna found amusing. The nice thing about children was that they were honest. There really wasn't anything interesting about Tenley and her companions, and the kids knew it.

"Tenley!" one of her sisters cried as she dashed forward.

She was shorter than Tenley, and her blond hair was cut in a stacked bob, but her eyes were the same vivid blue and her smile just as engaging.

"Ally," Tenley said as she hugged her sister tight. "You cut your hair. It looks so pretty."

"Well, better than it did with fistfuls of strained peas in it, at any rate." Ally laughed.

Brenna had met Ally, Tenley's youngest sister, a few times. She was the only one in the family who was proud of Tenley's shop, and she popped in every now and again to visit.

A handsome man in dress slacks and a sweater joined them. In his arms was a chubby baby who looked to be about nine months old.

"Baby Franny," Tenley said. "My, she's gotten big. Hi, Josh."

The man smiled and gave Tenley a hug. Then he reached past her to shake Matt's hand. "Josh Landry, Ally's husband."

"Matt Collins. Nice to meet you," Matt said. "This is Brenna, Tenley's business partner."

Brenna gave a smile and a wave.

"Josh, this is the paper artist I told you about," Ally said. "I love your work, Brenna. You're very talented."

"Thank you," Brenna said. "You're very kind."

"Not at all," Ally said. "In fact, I'm going to want to commission some things for Franny's room when we make it over to a big girl's room."

"Oh, yes, your little shop," another sister said as she approached. Judging by her superior tone, she was Carrie, the oldest. "How's that going?"

She buzzed the air near Tenley's cheek in what Brenna supposed was meant to be a kiss. She had dark hair and broad features, quite the opposite in looks from Tenley and Ally.

Brenna glanced at Tenley's parents, who were sitting in wing chairs by the fire. Carrie looked just like their mother, not unattractive but more handsome than pretty, whereas Tenley and Ally seemed to share

194

their father's fair complexion and finer features.

"It's going very well, thank you," Tenley said.

A tall, thin older man, looking very harried with a five-year-old clinging to his hand and whining for another piece of candy, approached.

"Ask your mother," he snapped, and handed the boy off to Carrie.

"Yes, yes, go have another, but don't spoil your dinner," Carrie said.

The last sister came over and stood next to Carrie. She didn't even bother to give Tenley an air-kiss. She merely glowered.

Brenna didn't think it was her sour expression that made her the least attractive of the four sisters, but it certainly didn't help.

"I can't believe you brought strangers to the family dinner," she hissed. "That's so like you, Tenley. You never think of anyone but yourself."

"I'm sorry you feel that way, Evie," Tenley said, but it was clear from her tone that she did not really care one little bit about what Evie thought.

Evie sniffed and tossed her mouse brown hair over her shoulder. Like Carrie, she had their mother's broad features, but what appeared strong and well chiseled on Carrie only overwhelmed Evie, giving her a doughy, overindulged appearance.

"Come on, let's get this over with," Tenley said, and she led Matt and Brenna over to her parents.

As they approached, her father looked up from the newspaper he was reading and her mother let her needlepoint fall into her lap. Brenna didn't know if Tenley had told them exactly who she was bringing to dinner, but judging by the looks of surprise on their faces, Brenna was betting no.

"Mother, Father," Tenley said, "I'd like to introduce you to Matt Collins and Brenna Miller. They are my guests for dinner."

Matt held out his hand to Mr. Morse. There was a slight hesitation before Mr. Morse took it and they shook.

"Welcome to our home," Mrs. Morse said. She sounded perfectly gracious, the consummate hostess.

"Thank you for having us," Brenna said.

An awkward silence ensued until Mrs. Morse glanced at Tenley. Her eyes narrowed. "You look pale, dear; are you feeling quite well?"

"Oh, I'm fine." Tenley gave her a small smile. "We're just crazy busy at the shop with leaf peepers. Right, Brenna?"

"Yeah, we're really raking it in," Brenna

quipped.

Matt and Tenley laughed, and so did Ally and Josh, but no one else seemed to get it. Brenna sighed. She hated to see a good pun go to waste.

"It's good to see you, Father," Tenley said. "Is there any news on who killed Uncle Harvey?"

Mr. Morse glanced at Matt and Brenna. "I hardly think this is the time to discuss this, Tenley."

She opened her mouth to respond, but the double doors were abruptly opened and Mrs. Winslow announced that dinner was served.

Mr. Morse rose and gestured to Mrs. Morse to lead. He followed her, and the rest of the family fell in behind them. Carrie and Evie followed their parents with their spouses in tow, leaving Ally and Tenley to bring up the rear.

The children were whisked away into another room by two nannies. Ally seemed the only mother reluctant to let go of her child, but the nanny smiled at her and re-assured her that she would come and get her if Franny cried.

"We don't have a nanny," Ally said to Tenley and Brenna. "I just love her so much. I don't want to share her with anyone. Is that terrible?"

"I think it's wonderful," Tenley said. She squeezed her sister's arm. "Franny is lucky to have you both."

Ally smiled and wrapped her hand around her husband's elbow. They made their way down the hall to another set of double doors, which opened into a large dining room.

Brenna felt her own upbringing come back at her in a rush. The same place settings with a confusing amount of china and silver, cloth napkins, and crystal glasses cluttered the table. There was a large portrait of a stern-looking man sporting a curled mustache and wearing a stiff-looking suit hanging on one wall, and on the opposite was a delicate-looking woman, with a pouf of blond hair on her head and wearing a silk dress that buttoned all the way up to her throat. Brenna was guessing these were the original Morses for whom the town was named.

Although the table was large, Brenna couldn't help but be aware that she was the odd number at the table. She sat between Matt and Josh, however, and felt fairly well insulated.

Mrs. Winslow was joined by two other young women to serve the family dinner.

They started with soup, a butternut squash seasoned with nutmeg, salt, and pepper. It was delicious. Then they moved on to salad. While the girls served new dishes and collected empty plates, the room maintained a steady buzz of chatter, most of which pertained to the weather and events in the town.

Despite the delicious food, Brenna could feel the tension in her shoulders increasing as she forced herself to smile and nod at every mundane comment thrown her way.

Yes, it was cold for October. No, no snow yet. Yes, the fire department did get a new fire engine. It was yellow and not the traditional red. No one was quite sure how they felt about it yet, but there had been grumblings about getting it painted.

Evie, who was sitting directly across from Brenna, signaled for her wineglass to be filled again. Brenna saw her husband put a restraining hand on her arm, but she shook him off and gestured for Mrs. Winslow to fill it almost to the brim.

Brenna glanced at Tenley's parents, but given that they were at opposite ends of the table, she didn't think they had a very clear view of Evie.

"So," Evie said, leaning forward. "I hear you're quite the body magnet, Brenna."

Brenna lowered her fork. She didn't know if she was supposed to respond, since it hadn't really been a question, but she didn't want to get caught with a mouthful of food if it turned out she was supposed to say something.

"Evie." Her husband said her name in a warning tone, but she ignored him.

"Well, what do you have to say about that, Brenna?" Evie asked. "I would be mortified if I had such a reputation, but that's me."

Tenley looked as if she were ready to throw a fork at her sister, but Brenna didn't want to be the cause of familial discord, so she said, "People talk. There's not much you can do about that."

"Yes, but you have been the one to find not one but three bodies in Morse Point, a town that hadn't seen a murder in over fifty years before you came here. I'm surprised Chief Barker doesn't bring you in for questioning."

Brenna took a small sip from her water glass. She really didn't want to cause a scene, but Evie was bringing it on herself.

"I'm sorry," she said, "but what exactly are you trying to say?"

"Nothing," her husband said. "I'm sure she meant nothing. Right, Evie?"

"Wrong," Evie snapped at her husband.

"I think I have every right to question what sort of person my sister has brought to the family dinner. You are a guest in our home. I would think you would want to explain your propensity for getting mixed up in all sorts of sordid situations, wouldn't you?"

"Now, just a minute, Evie," Tenley said, her voice low with warning. "Brenna is my friend. She has done nothing wrong, and I expect you to treat her cordially, as you would the Queen of England if she were invited to dinner."

"Oh, what's the matter?" Evie snarled. "Precious Tenley can't have anyone question her friend?"

"Evie, really," Carrie, the oldest sister, cut in brusquely. "You are being unconscionably rude."

"I'm being rude? I'm not the one who dragged her ignorant high school boyfriend here for Sunday dinner."

"Here we go," Matt muttered to Brenna.

"Evelyn." Mrs. Morse addressed her daughter in a tone that cracked like a whip and did not allow for arguing. "You will apologize to our guests at once."

Evie stared at Matt and Tenley. "Fine. I'm sorry you're a part of my sister's life and therefore now a part of my life."

"Evelyn!" Mr. Morse's voice rumbled

across the table like rolling thunder, causing Brenna to jump. Evie was not to be deterred, however.

"What's next, Sis? Are you going to get knocked up and marry the bartender?"

The entire room went quiet. As if Evie finally realized that she had gone too far, she leaned back in her chair, refusing to meet anyone's gaze, and sipped her wine.

"I apologize for my wife," Evie's husband said. She opened her mouth to protest, but he said, "Don't!"

Then he reached over and pried the glass of wine out of her hand. They stared at each other with a look of loathing so potent it was almost tangible.

"It's all right," Matt said in his soothing bartender's voice. Brenna had seen him talk many a drunk into a cab with that voice. "I'm sure she just said what everyone else is thinking."

"No, Matt, I'm sorry. But it's not all right. It's none of their business what goes on between you and me," Tenley said. "And as people who pride themselves on their good manners, I expected better of them. I'm sorry."

"But we're your family," Mr. Morse protested. Just then Mrs. Winslow came in with the next course, and everyone fell silent.

After they had all been served and she left, Mr. Morse continued. "It is our business who you get involved with because we care about you."

"Do you? Do you really?" Tenley asked. "Because you recently tried to set me up on a date with a man who is already involved with another woman."

"What?" Ally asked. "Who?"

"Dad's new vice president, Brian Steele," Tenley said.

"But he's so . . ." Ally paused, looking for the right words.

"Boring?" Brenna supplied.

"Well, yeah," Ally said.

"What do you mean he's involved with someone?" Mrs. Morse asked. "He never gave any indication that he was seeing anyone."

"Well, he is," Tenley said. "And she's one of the most disagreeable people I've ever had the misfortune to meet, although Evie is giving her a run for her money. Oh, and I think she was involved in Uncle Harvey's murder."

"Who? Evie?" Mrs. Morse blinked.

"No, Siobhan Dwyer," Tenley said.

"Who is that?" Mrs. Morse asked.

"She's the woman dating Brian."

"My new vice president?" Mr. Morse asked.

"The same," Tenley said.

"He's involved with Siobhan, who is my neighbor," Brenna said. "But they both deny it, even though Tenley and I saw them together."

"What do you know about Brian Steele?" Tenley asked her father. "How long has he worked for you? Where did he come from? What would he have to gain from you losing the company?"

"I don't know," Mr. Morse said. He looked confused, as if they were firing information at him too fast for him to process. "How does this have anything to do with who you're dating?"

"Given that you wanted me to dump Matt for Brian, I'd say it has a lot to do with it," Tenley said.

Mr. Morse's fair complexion grew blotchy, but Brenna couldn't tell if it was anger or embarrassment making it so.

"What makes you think this Siobhan woman or Brian have anything to do with Harvey's murder?" Mrs. Morse asked.

"Maybe it's just coincidence, but don't you think it's odd that Siobhan shows up to live in one of the Morse Point Lake cabins, Uncle Harvey is found dead in the woods around the lake, and Brenna and I see Brian, who is fairly new to your company, leaving Siobhan's cabin early one morning?"

"I'm sure there's a reasonable explanation," Mr. Morse blustered.

"Yes, they killed Uncle Harvey and are trying to pin it on you," Ally said.

All eyes turned to her.

"Well, that's what you're saying, isn't it?" she asked Tenley.

"We don't know," Tenley said. "We can't seem to get any background on either Brian or Siobhan. That's why I need you to tell me everything you know about him, Father."

"I am still unclear," Mr. Morse said. "How does this have anything to do with who you're dating?"

"It doesn't," Tenley said. "Who I date is my business and my business alone. I need you to find out from your personnel people anything they can about Brian Steele. Something isn't right there, and Brenna and I both agree that he may be the key to finding out what Siobhan's connection to Uncle Harvey is."

"I can't —" Mr. Morse protested, but Tenley cut him off.

"Of course you can. You're the boss."

She turned to Matt and smiled. He returned it and said, "Done?"

"Yes, I think I am." Tenley rose from her seat. "If you'll excuse us, I think my boyfriend and I are going to leave now."

Matt rose and walked her to the door. The entire family sat with their mouths agape. At the door, Matt turned around and said, "Thanks for dinner. Sorry we didn't make it to dessert. Oh, and for the record, I'm not just a bartender. I actually own the Fife and Drum and have for the past five years now."

If Tenley's family had been speechless a few minutes ago, they were now frozen in shock. Brenna watched them go, knowing that they would take Matt's car and she could follow in her Jeep. She saw Mrs. Winslow come through the doors with a tray full of crème brûlée. Yeah, she'd be right behind them, after she had her dessert.

CHAPTER 16

Evie looked at Brenna in disgust, as if she could not believe the breach of etiquette that Brenna was committing by staying when Tenley had left.

Brenna didn't care. Other than Ally and her husband, she didn't have the warm fuzzies for anyone seated in this room. They reminded her a little bit too much of her own pretentious parents and the life she'd shared with them in Boston.

She smiled graciously as Mrs. Winslow put her dessert in front of her. She did not wait for the others but picked up her spoon, ready to dig in. Crunchy crystallized sugar had to be broken through before she could get to the thick custard dessert underneath. It was divine.

After several more mouthfuls, when everyone else at the table had joined her, Brenna turned her attention to Mr. and Mrs. Morse. Now she would say what she had come to say.

"Are you aware, Mr. Morse, that Tenley asked me to help her find Harvey Lester's killer because she is afraid that you will be wrongly convicted?"

Mr. Morse slowly lowered his spoon. Brenna expected him to yell at her for her impertinence, but he didn't.

"No, I was unaware of that," he said. "But since I am innocent, she needn't trouble herself any further."

"I would say the same, but I'm afraid Tenley is a bit too protective of you to be put off," Brenna said. "So, here is how you are going to make it easy for her."

Mr. Morse glanced at her with one eyebrow raised. Brenna saw Ally's eyes widen, and she was quite sure no one generally spoke to Mr. Morse with such authority in his own home.

"You are quite blunt, Ms. Miller," Mr. Morse said.

"Oh, I haven't even begun," Brenna said. And she heard Josh mutter, "Go get him."

Brenna took one last bite of her dessert before she rested her spoon on the side of the dish. "You are going to gather all of the information you have on Brian Steele. You will then give it to Tenley, so that she and I can figure out what his relationship with

Siobhan Dwyer is and if they have a connection to Lester's death."

"If what you say is true, I have attorneys who can check into Brian's background."

"Yes, but can they check into Siobhan as efficiently as I can?" Brenna asked.

"I don't think it's appropriate for two young ladies to involve themselves in such matters," Mrs. Morse said. "It is better left to the police."

"I agree, but your daughter for some unfathomable reason cares too much about her family to let it go," Brenna said. Her tone made it clear that she couldn't imagine why Tenley would feel this way about this lot.

She rose from her seat. She was done here. She headed toward the door but then spun around to look at them. She realized she had one more thing to say.

"Do you have any idea how remarkable your daughter is?" she asked. "She saved me when I was completely adrift by offering me a job in her shop and helping me move to Morse Point. She runs an incredibly successful business, and she is beloved by everyone in town. And why wouldn't she be? She volunteers her time with the elderly and at-risk youth. She gives three hundred percent of herself to everyone she meets

209

without even being asked."

Brenna glanced around the table. Evie looked petulant, Carrie thoughtful, and Ally grateful. Mr. and Mrs. Morse were both staring at the tabletop — whether in shame or denial, Brenna couldn't tell, but she really didn't care.

"You should be proud of her and of who she is," Brenna said. "And if she has chosen to be with Matt Collins, you should count yourself lucky that she has found a person to spend her life with who is as good as she is and who loves her so very much."

Brenna took a step back toward the door. "Thank you for dinner. Please tell Mrs. Winslow it was excellent. I'll be in touch."

With that, Brenna swept from the dining room. Wow, a dramatic exit and she hadn't even tripped. Of course, now she had no idea where she was in the house or how to get out. Damn. She really did not want to go back and ask for directions, nor did she want to wander aimlessly and have the family find her.

"Psst," a voice hissed from farther down the hall, and Brenna followed the sound.

Mrs. Winslow stood there with her coat and purse. Her eyes were a bit misty as she helped Brenna into her coat. "Well said, miss, well said."

"Thank you," Brenna said. "Dinner was delicious."

Mrs. Winslow bowed her head in acknowledgment as she held the door for Brenna. The day had grown even colder and grayer since Brenna had arrived, but she was not unhappy to leave the austere estate behind her as she made her way to her cozy little home.

Brenna arrived at her cabin just as it was getting dark. The chill in the air made her burrow down deeper into her coat. Winter was coming fast now. Pretty soon the lake would freeze over and the snow would begin to fall. She thought about the shift in her relationship with Nate. She liked the idea of sitting by the fireplace in her cabin with Nate on one side and Hank on the other, talking about baseball or brownies or not talking at all.

She stepped up onto her porch and saw that the lights were on in Siobhan's cabin. Maybe it was time to go to the source. She strode over to her neighbor's without pausing to think about what she'd say once she got there; she just wanted some information to help out her friend. Maybe if she played nice with Siobhan, she'd get it.

She knocked on the door, but there was

no answer. She knocked again. Nothing. On impulse she tried the doorknob. It turned, and with a push the door swung open. Brenna wrestled with the moral dilemma of entering a place uninvited for about a nanosecond before she stepped inside.

"Hello?" she called. There was no answer.

She would just take a tiny peek around. Surely that couldn't hurt anyone. The house was sparsely decorated with the barest of furnishings: a couch, a coffee table, no television, just a laptop on the coffee table. It gave the impression that Siobhan would not be staying long. Not surprisingly, this did not cause Brenna to feel too badly. Not one little bit.

She checked the laptop, but it was off. She didn't think she should linger long enough to boot it up and check out what files Siobhan had, although she was curious.

She scanned the rest of the living area and then moved on to the bedroom. She wondered if Siobhan had taken Tenley's ring. Would she ever get another chance to search for it? Several boxes were scattered across the top of the bureau. One held makeup. One held several different perfumes. The largest held jewelry.

Brenna opened the top and found a tangle of earrings. She rifled through it but didn't see any rings. The bottom seemed awfully high and she wondered if there was more than one container. Sure enough, she lifted out the part that held the earrings and found another section full of necklaces and some rings. She checked through these as well, but still no emerald ring.

She replaced the lid and opened the dresser drawers. The clothes were neatly folded. There weren't many of them. The closet showed the same, a few dresses, a few pairs of shoes, but nothing that gave the impression that she would be here for very long.

Brenna walked through the bedroom, looking for personal effects. There were none — no photographs, no journals, nothing to tell her who Siobhan Dwyer was or where she came from.

Frustration clawed at her. There had to be something here, something that would give her a lead. She wandered back to the main room.

She saw Siobhan's art supplies set up in the corner. Her easel and drawing table were littered with work. Her years working in an art gallery made Brenna curious, so she stepped closer to study the work.

Siobhan worked in a variety of mediums. Brenna saw a charcoal sketch that depicted

Siobhan's face, but where her hair should be a large bird was perched. Several paintings were stacked against the wall, all self-portraits. In vibrant tones, Siobhan was depicted angry, and sad, and one looked disturbingly like she was dead.

Other than the self-portraits there were just a few landscapes and fruit bowls. Sadly, no portraits of either Mr. Lester or Brian Steele were to be found.

Something bothered Brenna about the portraits but she couldn't quite figure out what. She leaned closer to study them but heard a footstep on the front porch that made her heart pound in her chest. Siobhan was home. Uh-oh, Brenna wasn't a good enough liar to explain this.

Brenna quickly stepped toward the back door. Siobhan's cabin was laid out the same as hers, so she cut through the small kitchen and swiftly opened the back door. Just as the front door was opening, she shut the back door and quietly slipped across the yard to the back of her own cabin.

It was fully dark now, and she didn't think Siobhan could see her if she happened to look out her window, but still, Brenna skirted the edge of the trees, hoping to blend in with the foliage.

She was almost at her own back door

when a hand reached out of the darkness and grabbed her arm. Brenna opened her mouth to scream but another hand clamped over her mouth. She tried to gauge where her assailant's privates were so she could hit him with a crushing blow, but a familiar voice interrupted the thought.

"Brenna, it's me; don't scream."

Nate lowered his hand and she spun around to be sure it was him and not a trick.

"Oh, phew," she said. She bent over and put her hand over her pounding heart. The rush of panic had made her dizzy, and she sucked in great gulping breaths as she tried to calm down. "What are you doing skulking around out here?"

"I might ask you the same," he said. "I was looking for Hank."

Brenna turned and unlocked the back door to her cabin.

"I was snooping around Siobhan's cabin," she said.

They entered her kitchen and she flicked on the light switch.

"There is something not right about her," Brenna said. "I can't put my finger on it, but I know there's something wrong."

"I'm getting the same feeling," Nate agreed. "I still haven't heard from the friend who requested she stay here."

"Is that like your friend?"

"No, he's very reliable," Nate said. "I don't like this."

"Me neither."

A bark sounded from outside and Nate crossed the living area to open the front door for Hank. As soon as he cracked the door, Hank came bounding in to greet Brenna, dropping his tennis ball at her feet so he could give her a wet, slobbery kiss. He wasn't alone.

Standing on the porch was Siobhan. She was twirling a measuring cup in her hand and looking very put out.

"Hi, I was wondering if I could borrow a cup of sugar? Since you're a baker and all I figured you'd have some."

"Uh, sure," Brenna said. She tried not to look at Nate, not wanting to show her surprise. Did Siobhan know she had been over at her cabin? Had she seen her? Was the sugar just a ploy to come over and snoop herself?

Siobhan handed her the measuring cup and jumped back when Hank jumped up and tried to lick her. She gave him a very stern, "No."

Hank was undeterred and tried again. Siobhan moved so that a chair was between her and Hank.

Brenna poured the sugar from her stash in the pantry and was turning around to hand it to Siobhan when it hit her, the thing that had been bothering her about the artwork in her cabin. It was so obvious.

"You really have to give him something else to play with if you want him to behave," Brenna said. She placed the sugar on the counter and scooped up Hank's tennis ball from the floor. "Here, catch!"

Brenna tossed the ball at Siobhan, who caught it in her right hand. Nate opened the front door and said, "Throw it this way."

Siobhan tossed it out the door and Hank went bounding after it with a triple-twist leap of delight.

Brenna held out the sugar to Siobhan, who took it in both hands. Still, Brenna was sure. She opened her mouth to speak, but Nate cut her off.

"It's really dark out there," he said. "Let me walk you home."

Brenna looked at him and he gave a slight shake of his head. Had he figured it out, too?

"Thanks," Siobhan said with a flirty grin. Brenna tried not to let it bother her.

She watched the door shut behind them and then she began to pace. She assumed Nate would be coming back. As the minutes ticked by, she opened the door to peek out but found only Hank waiting with his ball in his mouth and his tail thumping against the porch floorboards.

"Come in," she said.

He trotted in, dropped his ball, and slurped out of the bowl of water she kept on the floor for him.

She opened her refrigerator and took out a cheesecake she had baked the day before. It was light and fluffy with a graham cracker crust. Just what her pensive mood needed.

She gave Hank a rolled-up piece of turkey lunch meat as she dug a plastic basket of strawberries out of the bottom drawer. She cut up the strawberries and put them in a bowl and sprinkled them with sugar. Then she fished a can of whipped cream out of the refrigerator and placed it on the counter. As if on cue, there was a knock on the front door, and then Nate walked in as Hank exploded in a frenzy of barking and wagging.

Nate looked at the counter and grinned. "Cheesecake?"

"It helps me think," Brenna said.

"Me, too," he said. He took a seat as Brenna handed him a plate and a fork. "Now, what were you about to say to Siobhan before I redirected?"

"So you did do that on purpose."

"I figured we should talk about it first and not be too hasty in case there's a smarter way to play it," he said.

"Probably wise," she said, although she did feel a bit chagrined. "When I was in her cabin earlier, I noticed something about her artwork but it didn't register until later."

Nate had dished them each a healthy slice of cheesecake, spooned strawberries on them, and was now topping them with whipped cream. "What was it?"

"The hatching marks on her sketches descend from left to right."

Nate was silent for a moment and then said, "But she caught Hank's ball in her right hand."

"Exactly."

"So, her artwork is left-handed but she's right-handed."

"Not terribly likely, don't you think?"

"Whoa," Nate said.

They sat silently mulling this bit of information while they finished off their cheesecake.

"She's a fraud," Brenna said. "If she lied about being an artist, she probably lied about everything else. I'd place money on the fact that she knew Lester. His daughter said something about his embarrassing midlife crisis. What if Siobhan was his midlife crisis?"

"You don't like her," Nate said. "Don't you think your dislike of her might be clouding your judgment?"

"No," Brenna said and cut herself another piece of cheesecake. Nate motioned for seconds as well, and she loaded them up with strawberries and whipped cream.

"If she killed Lester, why is she still here?" he asked.

"Maybe she expects a big chunk of his inheritance," Brenna said.

"If she's mentioned in his will," Nate said. "If she isn't, she'll get squat."

"If that's the case and you were the wife about to be left for her, wouldn't you want her to get squat?" Brenna asked.

"You think Mrs. Lester did him in before he could change his will?"

"It would be a motivator, but she has an alibi," Brenna said.

"I think we need to share this with Chief Barker."

"He's going to be irked with me," she said.

"He's always irked with you; you should be used to it by now."

"I suppose. I'll go see him tomorrow."

"Promise?"

"Yes."

Nate picked up their plates and rinsed them in the sink before putting them in her compact dishwasher. Brenna tried not to dwell on how right it felt to have him here in her kitchen with her.

Hank wagged his way over to them. He had his ball in his mouth and was obviously ready to go out and play again.

Brenna rubbed his ears as she walked them to the door.

"There's one more thing," Nate said. He turned to face her at the door. "We need to talk."

"Isn't that what we just did?" she asked.

"Not about the murder," he said. "About us."

CHAPTER 17

"Us?" Brenna repeated.

Oh no, was this where he gave her the I-like-you-as-a-friend spiel and that kiss the other day was just a reaction to the heat of the moment, yada yada, blah blah? She tried to brace herself for the crushing blow, but a surge of adrenaline caused the blood to rush into her ears, making it hard to hear.

"I like you," he said. "A lot."

Brenna swallowed past the lump in her throat.

"And I think we —" he began, but she interrupted in a fit of panic and said, "should just be friends."

"Really?" he asked. He looked surprised and a bit bewildered. "I was thinking we should go on a real date, but if you don't want to, that's okay."

"No!" she said more loudly than she had intended, making them both jump. She took a deep breath. "That is, I'd love to go on a date with you."

His gray eyes scrutinized her face and then crinkled at the corners when he smiled. "Does that mean you don't think we should just be friends?"

Brenna wondered if there was a flash point of humiliation where a person would just spontaneously combust from embarrassment. Probably not; that would be too easy.

"No, I just . . ." Her voice trailed off, and she almost left it at that, but then she figured he deserved the truth. If there was going to be anything worth having between them, then it needed a nice foundation of honesty. "I was afraid that was what you were going to say, so I made a preemptive strike."

"That's just silly talk," he said. "Just friends — as if. Pick you up tomorrow at seven?"

"Sounds perfect," she said.

He leaned close and gave her one swift kiss before he stepped out the door. Hank wagged after him, as if delighted with this sudden turn of events. Brenna was surprised she wasn't wagging herself. She pressed her fingers to her lips, which were still buzzing from the contact with his. A date? With Nate? She must be dreaming, and for once she didn't want to wake up.

■ ■ ■ ■

Luckily, the next day was her day off, so after stopping by Stan's Diner, she made her way over to the police station with a steaming latte-to-go in her hand. Stan had molded her froth into an autumn leaf dusted with nutmeg. Brenna had hated to put a plastic lid on it, but she didn't want to risk spillage.

She crossed the town green with an easy stride. She enjoyed the nip of cold air against her cheeks, the crunching sound of the fallen leaves under her feet, and the peaty smell of the earth as the same fallen leaves began to decompose on the ground. Autumn was being nudged aside by winter, and it would not be long before all the leaves were gone and the first snowfall came to call.

Halfway across the green, she spied Preston from the inn, leading his group of leaf peepers around the square.

She saw Julie and Suede, Jan and Stan in matching zipper vests, Paula, and Lily and Zach. The whole crew was out.

"Hi, everyone," Brenna greeted them.

"Well, look at you," Preston said. "You are glowing today. What's the occasion?"

"Frigid temperatures," Brenna said. She had no intention of telling Preston about her date with Nate. It'd be all over town before she made it to the police station.

"Uh-huh," he said. It was clear that he didn't believe her.

"What is the group doing today?" she asked.

"Well, it's our last day, so I am taking them on a walking tour of the town."

Brenna fell into step beside Julie and her son.

"We're going to see the graveyard," Suede said. He looked more animated at the prospect of seeing the historic resting place of the dead than he had at any other aspect of his trip.

Julie shook her head. "I suppose I should have taken him on a tour of cemeteries instead of changing leaves. Who knew?"

"Boys," Brenna said with a shrug. "Speaking of, how was your date?"

"Oh, are you sure you want to know?" Julie asked. "I mean, I didn't know you and Dom were a thing, and I don't want to come between anything."

"Julie, relax," Brenna said. "We're just friends."

"Are you sure?" Julie asked.

Brenna felt a small twinge of regret, but

then she remembered her date with Nate. "Yes, I'm positive."

"Well, okay, then." Julie huffed out a big breath. "I really like him. He's funny and handsome and kind, and Suede just thinks he's all that. I don't know if there's any kind of future, since it would have to be a long-distance kind of thing, but it was really nice to go out with someone who made me feel special. You know?"

"Yeah, I do," Brenna said.

"I think he has feelings for you," Julie said. Then she bit her lip as if afraid she'd said too much.

"We did date once," Brenna said. She wasn't going to lie to Julie. She liked her and considered her a new friend. "But I care for someone else. I think Dom just hasn't met the one yet. Who knows, maybe it's you."

"Wouldn't that be something?" Julie asked. She sounded optimistic, as if there hadn't been anyone special in her life for a while. Brenna hoped that if things didn't work out with Julie and Dom, then she would find someone worthy of her. She was a lovely lady.

Brenna glanced at the group that had fanned out around the park. Lily and Zach were leaning up against a tree, staring into each other's eyes.

"I miss that," Julie said, following Brenna's gaze. "That feeling that another person is your other half."

Brenna's gaze moved from the young couple to Jan and Dan, who were holding hands while they strolled through the colorful trees. She watched the way Dan tipped his head toward Jan to listen to her speak and the way she laughed at his jokes with abandon. She would be hard-pressed to determine which of these two couples was more in love.

"It is a beautiful thing to find your soul mate," Brenna said.

"I don't believe in that," Paula said as she joined them. "I don't think love lasts. Sure, they're all happy today, but all relationships end badly. Either someone leaves or someone dies; either way there is no escaping the fact that heartbreak is inevitable."

"I suppose you're right," Brenna said. "But I wouldn't give up the joy of falling in love just because the ending is a little rough."

"You're braver than me," Paula said.

Julie smiled at them and drifted off to join her son, who was bugging Preston to go to the cemetery right now.

"I don't know if it's bravery or stupidity

to fall in love," Brenna said. "I just know it's fun."

Paula made a sound of disbelief and Brenna turned to study her. She really was a lovely girl in a very understated way.

"Are you excited to be going home?" she asked.

"No, this is such a lovely town," Paula said. "I can't believe how at home I feel. I'm just waiting for the library to open, so I can read up on its history."

"Oh, I'm glad you like it," Brenna said. "I've only lived here a couple of years, but I can't imagine living anyplace else. And Preston and Gary really do make their inn feel like a second home, don't they?"

"They do," she said. "When I get back home to New York, I'm going to tell everyone I know about this place."

"Just do us a favor and don't mention the body in the woods," Brenna said. "I can't imagine that would boost our tourism."

"You never know," Paula said with a shiver of macabre delight. "Some people like that grisly sort of thing."

Brenna nodded. It must be nice to be young like Paula and think of death as just the next great venture. Brenna was old enough to be too aware of the finality of it all. Had Harvey Lester known when he entered those woods that he wouldn't be leaving? It gave her the shivers to think of it, and not in a good way.

It was nine o'clock now and as Paula and the others left to go, Brenna walked to the police station. It was still quiet this early in the day. She entered the main room and gestured to Officer DeFalco, who was on the phone, that she was going in back to talk to Chief Barker. DeFalco nodded for her to go ahead.

Chief Barker was sitting in his high-backed, rolling desk chair. He had a rod and reel in his hands and it looked as if he was trying to untangle a knot of fishing line.

"Morning, Chief," Brenna said. "Got a minute?"

"Got two," he said. "What can I do for you?"

"I wanted to talk to you about the Lester murder," she said.

"Why am I not surprised?" he asked. He ran a finger over his gray mustache and put the fishing reel down. "What's on your mind?"

Brenna took a deep breath and told him everything she had learned about Siobhan and that it wasn't just her but that Nate, too, felt there was something not right about her. She hoped that would add more weight to her argument.

"How is it you had such an opportunity to study Ms. Dwyer's work?"

"What do you mean?" she asked. Had she given away too much? She'd been very careful not to make it sound like she'd snooped around Siobhan's cabin, which of course she had.

Brenna was spared from answering, however, as the door banged open and there stood Tenley. Her eyes flashed blue fire and her stance was rigid, as if she were ready for combat.

"I demand an explanation," she said.

Brenna blinked. Tenley sounded exactly like her mother, Tricia. She'd heard her mimic her mother before — it was always good for a laugh — but this time she sounded serious and she looked furious.

Brenna glanced at Chief Barker to see how he was taking this. He glanced at Tenley and spoke slowly, as if she were perched on a fifty-foot ledge and intent on jumping.

"I know you're upset," he said.

"Upset?" she gasped. "I am more than upset. I am livid. How could you? How could you arrest my father for a crime he can't possibly have committed?"

"What?" Brenna whipped her head from Tenley to Chief Barker. "Is this true?"

Chief Barker heaved a sigh. "We got a tip. We found the murder weapon in the glove box of your father's Buick. We had no choice."

"A tip from who?"

"I'm not at liberty to divulge that information."

"You're not at liberty, or you can't because you don't know?" Tenley asked.

Chief Barker didn't answer.

"I knew it. It was anonymous, wasn't it?" Tenley pressed.

Chief Barker gave her a reluctant nod.

"But of course, don't you see, whoever killed Uncle Harvey is setting my father up."

"The investigation isn't over. If that's the case, then we'll find out who really did it."

"And in the meantime?" Tenley asked.

"Your father stays with us."

CHAPTER 18

Brenna steered Tenley back to Vintage
Papers. She was so rattled, Brenna was
afraid she'd walk out into traffic if she
wasn't led by someone else.

"I just can't believe this," Tenley said. "My
father would never do anything to harm
Uncle Harvey. How could the murder
weapon have been in his car? Someone must
have planted it."

No sooner had they shut the door behind
them than it was yanked open by Matt
Collins. Tenley glanced up at him and he
simply opened his arms wide. She stepped
into his embrace and it was as if the rest of
the world vanished.

Brenna figured Matt was really the only
one who could comfort Tenley right now.
She decided to give them some privacy and
left the shop, flipping the store's sign to
CLOSED and locking the door behind her.
She walked to her Jeep and decided to go

for a drive. Second to showering, driving was a great activity for thinking, especially when there was no specific destination in mind.

She didn't like the anonymous tip thing, and judging by Chief Barker's frown, he didn't, either. Still, it was not something that could be ignored.

Brenna wondered if the call from the tipster had been traced. Surely that would give them some information. She knew that Nate would tell her she was being paranoid, but she wondered if Siobhan was the one who had placed that call. If only she could prove that Siobhan had been having an affair with Lester, then she knew she could get the chief to investigate her more thoroughly.

As she motored out of town, she thought back to what Nate had said. If Siobhan was the killer, why was she still here? There had to be something in it for her.

Was she in his will? That would be motive. Had he backed out of their relationship and she killed him in anger? That would be a crime of passion, but why would she stick around? Maybe it was a combination of the two. Maybe she was in his will and he backed out of their relationship and she killed him, hoping she'd still get her chunk of his fortune. And if someone else got arrested for the murder, well, that would be the cherry on top.

Brenna had a feeling Nate would tell her that this was pretty far-fetched and it was her dislike of Siobhan that had her fixated on her as the murderer. Maybe. Or maybe she was on to something. There was only one way to find out. She needed to talk to Lydia Lester again and see if she knew anything about her husband's will.

Brenna arrived at the country club fifteen minutes later. She straightened her shoulders and walked in as if she were a member. The host at the doorway to the dining room gave her a once-over and Brenna wished she had dressed in something other than khakis and a sweater.

The badge on his shirt read TREVOR. He was tall and thin, with pinched features, as if he perpetually smelled something foul. Brenna hoped it wasn't her. The part in his light brown hair was as straight as a ruler's edge. He looked young, in his early twenties, and she wondered if he'd ever grow into his rather large nose and ears or if they would always appear two sizes too big.

"Hello, Trevor. I'm meeting Mrs. Lester," she lied. "Could you direct me to her?"

Trevor's demeanor changed into one of

obsequious good cheer. "Why, yes, of course. Please follow me."

They strode down a wide hallway past the bar Brenna remembered from her last visit to a large sitting room. Cushy leather chairs were scattered among antique tables. Newspapers and magazines were plentiful and a wide-screen television took up one corner of the room.

There were very few people in here this early in the day, but in one corner sat Lydia Lester. She had a travel magazine in one hand and a Bloody Mary in the other.

The wobbly expression on her face led Brenna to believe this was not her first cocktail of the day.

"Hi, Lydia." Brenna swept right up to her, giving Lydia no choice but to hug her back. "So good to see you again."

Lydia blinked at her as if trying to place her, and Brenna turned to Trevor and said, "Could you bring me one of whatever she's drinking and another for her? Thanks."

"I'll inform your server," Trevor said with a slight bow, letting Brenna know that he saw himself above the position of waitstaff.

She plunked down in the chair next to Lydia's and said, "So, what are we drinking to today?"

Fuzzy recognition lit Lydia's eyes and she

said, "Bernice, is that you?"

"Brenna, actually," she said.

"Bernice, Brenna, Brittany, whatever." Lydia waved her hand. "How the heck are you?"

"Doing well," she said. "And you? Still celebrating?"

"You'd better believe it," Lydia said. "I heard they arrested Rupert Morse this morning. I feel badly about that. I'm thinking I need to send him flowers or a casserole or something."

"Do you really think he did it?"

A waitress appeared with their drinks. Brenna expected Lydia to hold her tongue until the young girl left, but Lydia barely acknowledged the girl's presence.

"He must have," she said.

"Thank you," Brenna said to the waitress, who took away Lydia's empty glass as she left.

"Here's to a husband-free cruise," Lydia said and clinked her glass against Brenna's. "I'm going around the world on a boat. I'm going to sit in a lounger with my flag up and pickle myself on the rums of the Caribbean, the beers of Germany, and the plum wines of Japan."

"That's ambitious," Brenna said. "How long will you be gone?"

"A year, give or take," Lydia said.

"Can you afford that?" Brenna asked. "I mean, you have the estate to settle and all."

"That shouldn't be a problem," Lydia said. "I'm Harvey's wife. I know he left some smaller sums for the girls but the bulk of his estate goes to me."

"I hate to be indelicate," Brenna said. "But . . ."

She hesitated. She really hoped that Lydia was drunk enough for her to broach this subject without making her angry.

"But what? Don't stall now, dear," Lydia said. She clinked her glass against Brenna's again. "To wealthy widowhood."

"I heard, and I'm sorry to repeat it, that Harvey was having an affair," she said. "Aren't you afraid he may have left something to his mistress?"

Lydia sat up straight as if this thought had never occurred to her. She contemplated this as she took a healthy swig off of her drink.

"I would be concerned," she said, but then gave Brenna a sly smile. "But I found out about his little love muffin, oh, six months ago, and I very quietly and very carefully had him sign over ownership of the house, the cars, the vacation homes, and the joint bank accounts to me."

"How did you manage that?"

"Easy. He was so preoccupied with his new hobby that when I told him I needed his signature on some insurance papers, he never even bothered to look. What a dope. When he left me, the only thing he could take with him was a paper sack full of underwear."

"So, he actually left you?" Brenna asked. "When was that?"

"About a week before he died," Lydia said. "He tried to use the credit cards to book a room in a posh hotel in Milstead, but he was rejected. I'm sure it was a nasty shock for him to discover that his name had been removed from all of our accounts."

"What happened then?"

"Oh, the usual," Lydia said. "He called angry at first; then he tried to bargain. I'm sure he was in a panic because once his little tart found out he was broke, she'd leave him flat. He really had no choice but to try to sell his portion of the company to make enough money to keep his little chippie happy. He even tried to sell it to me. Ha!"

"What did you say to that?"

"I told him to get bent. I bore four children for that man. I worked while he went to school. I borrowed money from my parents to help him start his little business with Rupert Morse, and he thought he was just going to walk away from forty years of marriage and start over again with some young bit of fluff. Humph, not on my watch."

Brenna looked at the fire in Lydia's eyes and she wondered if she'd been wrong. If ever there was anyone with sufficient rage and a motive for Harvey's murder, it was Lydia. Just because she liked Lydia's spunk and zest for life, she couldn't overlook her as a prime suspect.

"Lydia, you didn't . . ." Brenna's voice trailed off. She wasn't sure how to ask this question.

"No, I didn't," Lydia said. She took a hearty swallow from her glass and smiled at Brenna.

"Didn't what?" Brenna asked.

"Murder my husband," Lydia said. "Chief Barker has asked me repeatedly, but the answer is no. Not that he didn't deserve it, but how would that be a satisfying revenge for his shenanigans? No, no, the absolute best revenge was going to be to live extraordinarily well and rub his stubby little nose in it for the rest of his life."

Lydia stared down into her glass and looked morose.

"What's wrong?" Brenna asked.

"Someone took that away from me," Lydia said in a small voice. "Someone took my daughters' father away from them. It isn't right, even if he was being a two-timing pig."

Lydia took another sip from her glass and shook off her melancholy like a duck flapping water off of its wings.

"So, what do you think of my travel plans?" she asked.

"Impressive."

"I thought so." Lydia tipped her head in acknowledgment. "Now with Rupert in jail and Harvey dead, I figure Tricia and I can sell off the company for a nice profit. She certainly deserves it after all these years with Rupert. Do you think she'd want to come on the cruise with me? Maybe I should invite her."

Brenna tried to wrap her brain around a picture of drunken Lydia and prim Tricia cavorting on a cruise around the world together. She couldn't get it to focus.

"I don't see Tricia leaving Rupert," she said.

"Don't be too sure," Lydia said. "If he gives me any trouble about selling the company, I fully intend to use his previous indiscretion against him and force him to agree."

"Indiscretion? Mr. Morse?"

"Indeed," Lydia said with a chortle.

Brenna opened her mouth to barrage Lydia with questions, but her daughter Kristin arrived, took one look at the two of them, and huffed in disgust.

"Mother, how could you?" she asked. "I told you we had to go to the funeral home today to make arrangements. I can't take you like this."

"So don't," Lydia said. She tried to down her drink before her daughter snatched it away, but Kristin was too quick for her. "As far as I'm concerned, your father can be cremated and stuffed in a coffee can to be taken out with the trash."

"I'm sorry, but are you a member here?" Kristin turned flashing eyes on Brenna.

"Bernice is my guest," Lydia said.

"Really? I thought her name was Brenna," Kristin said. A vein had begun to throb in her temple.

Brenna sensed this might be a good time to make a full retreat. "Would you look at the time? Gotta run. Great to see you again, Lydia. Keep in touch."

Brenna power walked out of the sitting room, without breaking her stride or looking back. She waved at Trevor as she passed, hoping she didn't look like she was running away, which she was.

She hurried across the parking lot to her Jeep and started down the winding road past the golf course and back to the main road. A brisk breeze was tickling the leaves out of the trees, and she felt as if she were driving through a shower of gold as she left the club behind her.

She couldn't help but mull over Lydia's words as she drove. What indiscretion could Mr. Morse possibly have in his past that Lydia could use to leverage his cooperation now? Maybe it was just wishful thinking or too many Bloody Marys on Lydia's part that made her think she had something on him.

Still, she had sounded awfully sure. Brenna would have liked to ask Tenley about it, but she suspected that would not go over well. Tenley may be at odds with her family over her business and her relationship with Matt, but she was still as loyal to them as the tide to the pull of the moon, and Brenna knew that she would never believe any ill of them, especially her father.

Who, then, could she ask? There was really only one choice. The Porter sisters knew everyone and everything that happened in Morse Point. If Brenna wanted to know if Lydia could really have some dirt on Mr.

Morse, then she had to run it by Ella and Marie.

The Porter sisters shared a small, butter yellow bungalow with green shutters and a white picket fence just off the center of town. Neat and tidy, their house was always immaculate inside and out.

Brenna rang the captain's bell that hung beside the front door.

"I've got it," came a voice from inside.

"No, I do," said another.

"It's my turn; you got it the last time."

"I did not."

The door was abruptly yanked open and two gray heads popped out.

"Brenna!" they said together. "Come in."

"I was just making some tea," Marie said. "Do you like Brie? I have some sesame crackers that are just perfect with a chunk of Brie."

"Oh, don't go to any trouble," Brenna said.

"It's no trouble." Marie waved her hand. "You two go sit. I'll be right there."

Ella led Brenna into a cozy front room. A small fire was crackling in the fireplace and a wooden worktable was in the center of the room, covered in newspaper with several pumpkins on top of that.

"Since you're here, you may as well pitch in to help," Ella said. "We're decoupaging these pumpkins."

"Really?"

"They can't have jack-o-lanterns in the children's wing at the hospital, so Marie and I thought we'd cover these with bats and spiders and bring them over to brighten the place up."

"That's a wonderful idea."

"You can borrow it if you want," Ella said. She sounded nonchalant, but Brenna could tell she was pleased with the praise.

Brenna picked out a chunky pumpkin and some cutouts of happy bats. She coated the back of the bat with glue and then used a sponge brush to press it into the creases of the pumpkin.

She could hear Marie rattling in the kitchen and she glanced at Ella. She had her head down and was trying to get a delicate spiderweb in place without ripping it.

"Ella, what happened to John Henry?" she asked. She hadn't realized she was going to ask until the words flew out of her mouth, but there it was, and there was no taking it back.

"What makes you ask?" Ella didn't seem surprised by the question and she didn't look up from her pumpkin.

"I don't know," Brenna said. "It's just that you two talk about him all of the time, and I can't help wondering . . ."

"He died," Ella said. Now she did look up at Brenna. "In 1966, in Vietnam."

"I'm sorry," Brenna said. Now she felt horrible for asking.

"It's been forty-four years since he died, and not a day goes by that I don't think of him," she said. She glanced toward the kitchen. They could hear Marie humming, and Ella leaned close to Brenna and said, "He asked me to marry him, and I said no. The next day he enlisted and I never saw him again."

There was no emotion visible on Ella's face, but Brenna could hear the regret in her voice.

"Does Marie . . . ?"

"Know that he asked me?" Ella guessed. "No. I never told her."

"But why did you say no? You obviously loved him, and he loved you."

"Because Marie was in love with him, too," she said. "I knew if I married him, it would break her heart. I couldn't do that to her."

Brenna felt as if all of the air had been sucked out of the room. Ella had said no to

245

the love of her life for her sister, and he had died. How did she live with that every day?

"Why did you tell me this now?" Brenna asked.

"Because some of the choices we make can't be undone," Ella said. "You're going to have an important decision to make — choose wisely."

Brenna looked back at her pumpkin. Great, no pressure.

"So, what brings you here, Brenna?" Marie asked as she entered the room, carrying a fully loaded tray of tea and crackers with Brie.

"Can't a friend just pop in to say hello?"

"Certainly," Ella said. "But that's not what you're doing. You're fishing for information."

"I . . . Oh, all right. I am," Brenna admitted.

Ella and Marie exchanged knowing glances, and Brenna wondered how many other people just stopped by the sisters' bungalow.

"Well, you've come to the right place," Marie said.

The three of them dished crackers and cheese onto their plates and then helped themselves to tea.

It was so warm and cozy here with the

Porter sisters and their pumpkins that Brenna almost forgot her mission.

"Well, spill it," Ella said. "What do you need to know?"

"I need to know what Rupert Morse's indiscretion was."

Ella and Marie gave her matching expressions of surprise. With their eyebrows raised and lips pursed, they looked like bookends.

"We can't help you," they said together.

CHAPTER 19

"What?" Brenna asked. "What do you mean? You two know everything about everyone. You have to know about this."

"We didn't say we didn't know about it," Marie said gently.

"We just can't tell you," Ella said.

Brenna took a sip of tea. She felt as if the earth was off its axis. There had been an indiscretion and the Porter sisters didn't want to share? Something was very wrong here.

"Why can't you tell me?" she asked.

"It was a long time ago," Ella said. "It's best forgotten now."

"How can you say that?" Brenna asked. "Listen, Lydia Lester is planning to sell Lester and Morse, Inc., and she said she'd use Mr. Morse's indiscretion to make him agree to selling if she must."

The Porter sisters gasped as one. Ella took a bracing sip of tea, and Marie popped a

Brie-covered cracker into her mouth.

"Well, that's hitting below the belt, even for Lydia," Ella said.

"Indeed," sniffed Marie. "Do you think Rupert will agree to sell?"

"What choice will he have?" Ella asked. "If he wants to keep his squeaky clean image intact, he'll have to agree."

Brenna glanced between the two of them. Were they really not going to tell her? This was maddening.

"Okay, I'm not leaving until you tell me what Mr. Morse could possibly have done," Brenna said. She slumped back in her chair and tried to look as if she was about to take root there.

The sisters looked at her. "Well, it'll be nice to have an extra pair of hands around the house," Ella said to Marie.

"Especially since we want to remodel the upstairs bathroom. She looks fit enough to do some tiling," Marie said. "I'll just call Sam Payson and tell him we won't be needing him after all."

"Oh, come on," Brenna said. "I need to know what happened if I am going to help Tenley solve Harvey Lester's murder and get her father out of jail."

"It is precisely because of Tenley that we can't tell you about Rupert," Marie said.

"We're trying to protect her," Ella said.

Brenna stuffed a cracker with a chunk of Brie on it into her mouth and chewed vigorously while she thought.

"What if I promise not to tell Tenley what you tell me?" she asked.

They exchanged another look.

"I don't know," Ella said doubtfully. "Tenley is your best friend."

"And this is really huge," Marie said. "I don't know if you'll be able to stop yourself."

"I can keep a secret," Brenna said. She looked at Ella. She leaned forward in her chair and placed her teacup back on the table. She put her right hand over her heart. "I swear that whatever you tell me I will not divulge to anyone, and I do mean anyone."

"Not Tenley," Ella said. "Or Nate."

"Or Dom," Marie added.

"You have my word. I won't even tell Hank," Brenna said.

"The dog?" Ella asked. "You may want to hold off on that promise. Because you're going to want to tell someone, and he doesn't seem the type to blab."

"Okay, okay, now tell me," Brenna pleaded.

"All right, it —" Ella began, but Marie interrupted, "Oh, no, I get to tell her."

"No, you don't. It's my turn," Ella said.

"How do you figure that?" Marie snapped. "We've never told anyone this before."

"You stole John Henry from me," Ella said with a sidelong look at Brenna. "You owe me."

"Oh, for heaven's sake, I did not," Marie said. "He loved me."

Brenna put her fingers to her temples. She was pretty sure she was going to have an aneurysm. "Stop it, both of you."

The sisters both whipped their heads in her direction.

"You can each tell me half of the story," she said. "Ella, you start."

Ella gave her sister a self-satisfied smirk. "It happened about twenty years ago."

"Twenty-four," Marie corrected.

"Fine, twenty-four," Ella said. "Lester and Morse, Inc., was one of the top companies in town, and the Morses and the Lesters were seen at all the town functions. They each had a passel of girls, you see, so the families were always together. Then we noticed that we were seeing less and less of Rupert."

"Poor Tricia, four girls and she was almost always alone," Marie clucked.

"Well, they said it was the business that was keeping him so busy, but Harvey was

251

still around, so we couldn't figure out why Rupert seemed to be doing all of the work."

"Then we saw her," Marie said.

"Hey, I wasn't finished with my half," Ella protested.

"Yes, you were; it's my turn now," Marie said. "Fair's fair."

"Humph." Ella sat back with her crackers and tea.

"You saw who?" Brenna asked, trying to get them back on track.

"Rupert Morse's secretary, Lynette Compton," Marie said in a stage whisper. "I remember exactly. I was having my annual exam when in came Lynette. She was pale and tired-looking and she threw up right on Dr. Piski."

Brenna looked at her. Obviously this was important, but she couldn't for the life of her figure out why.

"She was such a cute young thing," Ella said. "Tiny and blond, she was the complete opposite of Tricia, and not at all snooty."

"You could see why Rupert fell. Lynette was bubbly and fun, but he couldn't very well leave his wife and four girls, now could he?" Marie asked.

"Do you mean to tell me that Rupert Morse had an affair with his secretary?" she asked.

"Not just an affair," Marie said. "Lynette got pregnant with his child."

Brenna felt her jaw drop. Truly, she could not picture the stuffy Mr. Morse doing anything so completely out of character. "We are talking about Rupert Morse here? Tenley's father?"

"The same," Ella said. "Tricia found out, of course, and Lynette was sent away and forced to put the baby up for adoption."

"So, Tenley has a half sibling that she doesn't even know exists?" Brenna asked.

"Now you know why we didn't want to tell you," Marie said. "And you have to keep your promise. We adore Tenley and we don't want her to be hurt."

Brenna nodded. This would flatten Tenley on a lot of levels, and she didn't want to be the one who did that to her friend.

"Was the baby a boy or a girl?" she asked.

"No one knows," Marie said. "Lynette was bought off with a huge chunk of money and no one ever saw her again."

"The only people who know the truth are Rupert; Tricia; Lynette, of course; and us," Ella said.

"How is it that you two know this?" Brenna asked.

"I just happened to be in the hall, stretching my legs, when Dr. Piski told Lynette she was pregnant," Marie said. "I wasn't trying to listen, really."

"And then I saw Rupert pick her up from the doctor's office," Ella said. "So, we figured he was the father."

"Uh-huh," Brenna said. "If you're the only ones who know about this, how is it that Lydia knows?"

"There was a time when Lydia and Tricia were best friends," Ella said. "I wouldn't be surprised if Tricia told Lydia when it was happening. She probably needed the moral support."

"I feel like everything I have ever known about Rupert Morse is one big, fat lie," Brenna said. "It would kill Tenley to know that her father had an affair and a child that he sent away. If he could do all of that . . . Tell me the truth, do you think Rupert Morse killed Harvey Lester?"

The sisters were quiet for a long moment as they considered her question.

Finally, Marie said, "If Harvey did sell his half of the business to someone who planned to shut them down, then Rupert was about to lose everything."

"Which is a pretty solid motivation for murder," Ella said.

"But would he really be stupid enough to keep the murder weapon in his glove box?"

Brenna asked. "That just screams of a setup."

They sipped their tea and nibbled their crackers in silence, but no one could think of an answer to the larger questions of who killed Harvey Lester and who would set up Rupert Morse to take the fall?

Brenna thanked the Porter sisters for the tea and the information. The two ladies walked her to the door.

"You have to swear you won't tell Tenley," Marie said.

"The reason we've kept it such a secret all these years is to keep Tenley and her sisters from being needlessly hurt," Ella said.

"I promise," Brenna said. "She is suffering enough with her father being incarcerated. I definitely don't want to add to it."

Brenna drove into town and found a parking spot a few spaces down from the shop. She practiced keeping her face blank. She did not want to give Tenley anything to be suspicious about.

The bells jangled when she walked into the shop and she was surprised to find it empty. She walked into the break room to put her purse away and heard an awful retching noise coming from the bathroom.

"Tenley, are you all right?" she asked.

"Fine," Tenley called. The sound of flushing and water running came from the small bathroom, and then Tenley appeared, looking pasty and wan.

"Oh, sweetie." Brenna rushed forward and helped her into a chair. "You need to go home and get some rest. You are getting way too wiped out by all that is happening. I can take care of the shop."

"It's not Uncle Harvey's murder that has me wiped out," Tenley said.

"Is it your dad?" Brenna asked. "We'll get him out of jail, I promise."

Tenley pushed a lank section of hair aside and raised her face so that her eyes met Brenna's. "I'm pregnant."

CHAPTER 20

Brenna fell into the seat beside her. "Repeat, please."

Tenley gave her a small smile. "You heard right. I'm having a baby."

"Congratulations?" Brenna said and waited to see if Tenley laughed or cried. To her profound relief, Tenley laughed and hugged her.

"It's all right," she said. "It was a surprise, but Matt and I are very happy."

"I'm so glad," Brenna said.

"We're going to get married," Tenley said. "We'll have a small ceremony at the church and a gathering of friends and family at the Fife."

"It sounds lovely," Brenna said. "If there is anything I can do to help, just ask."

"Will you stand up for me?" Tenley asked. "I don't know how my family is going to take this, and I want someone up there with me who is actually happy for me."

"Done," Brenna agreed. She felt her throat squeeze tight, and her eyes grew damp. "Truly, I'm honored."

Tenley hugged her again. When she pulled back, Brenna looked at her friend and said, "Wow, a baby."

"Good word — *wow.*"

"Are you scared?" Brenna asked. "I mean, it's a huge life change."

Tenley looked thoughtful and then she smiled. "I feel as if I finally have the life I've always wanted."

Despite the pallor of her skin, there was a peacefulness about Tenley that Brenna had never seen before. It seemed that despite the chaos around her, she had discovered what mattered most in her life: Matt and their baby. Brenna was relieved. She couldn't think of anyone who deserved her heart's desire more.

"I'm so happy for you," she said. "Still, you look wiped out. Go home and take a nap. I'll watch the shop for the rest of today, so long as you don't mind if I close a bit early."

"You have someplace better to be than here?" Tenley asked.

"I do." Brenna stood and walked back into the shop. Tenley followed.

"Well, don't leave a girl hanging. What

258

could be better than this? A date? Do you have a date? That's it — you have a date!"

Brenna went over to the corner and hefted the small dresser she had salvaged the week before onto the worktable. She had sanded it down at home and smoothed out most of its dents and gouges. She had given it a base coat of dark olive green, which was finally dry. Now she needed to start working on her layout.

"I am not leaving until you tell me who your date is with," Tenley said.

The door opened halfway through Tenley's sentence, and they both started to see Dom Cappicola walk in.

"Date? Who has a date?" Dom asked.

Tenley looked at Brenna and gestured toward Dom with her head. Brenna shook her head no. Tenley made a small *oh* out of her mouth, and then her eyes went wide as she realized who the date must be with.

"Call me," she said. "Wardrobe must be discussed."

"Definitely."

"Promise."

"Okay, I promise. Now go and rest."

"Good to see you, Dom," Tenley said as she passed him on her way out.

"You, too," he said.

When the door closed behind her, he

looked at Brenna. "Something I said?"

She smiled. "No, she's feeling a little under the weather."

"So, you must be the one with the hot date then," he said. He was wearing a single-breasted black overcoat over a sweater and slacks. Per usual, he was emanating a raw power that made Tenley's cute little paper shop seem alarmingly combustible.

"Yes, I do have a date," she said.

"Finally," he said. "Williams is going to take you out and bore you to tears."

A surprised laugh burst from Brenna, and she clapped a hand over her mouth. Dom's dark brown eyes twinkled at her.

"It's so much easier to compete with a real person than the idea of a person. I think you and I will actually have a fighting chance once you go out with him and realize he's not all that."

"You think so?" she asked.

"Know so," he corrected. "Just you wait. You'll be begging me to take you out again."

"Uh-huh." She decided to change the subject. "I don't suppose you were able to find out anything about Lester and Morse?"

"Back to business," he said with a sigh. "No worries. I'll be waiting for your call tomorrow."

Brenna just shook her head.

"So, as we know, Lester was shopping around his portion of the company."

"Why didn't Morse just scrape up the money to buy him out?" Brenna asked.

"Well, the business hasn't been doing that well over the past few years, and the bank turned down Morse's request for a loan that would have let him buy Lester out."

He walked while he talked, stopping to examine the red armoire that was Brenna's largest piece to date.

"Did you do this?" he asked.

"A few years ago," she said.

He ran a finger over the paper cutouts of Louis XIV–era wigged gents and ladies strolling through lush gardens.

"It's brilliant," he said. "You should have your own studio."

Brenna shrugged. "This is enough for me."

He turned to face her, opened his mouth to say something, but then seemed to think better of it.

"What?" she asked.

"It'll keep," he said. He had a small smile playing on his lips as if she amused him, and Brenna realized that she had become quite fond of him over the past few months. Not for the first time she wondered if things would be different if she had met Dom before Nate. There was no way to know.

"I have another question for you," she said.

"Let 'er rip," he said.

"This is very hush-hush," she said. "You can't tell anyone."

"You have my word," he said. He moved to stand directly in front of her, and Brenna had to tip her head just slightly to look up at him.

"I need to know anything you can find out about the whereabouts of Lynette Compton, former secretary to Rupert Morse. She left Lester and Morse about twenty-four years ago."

Dom raised his eyebrows in surprise. "I'll use my contacts at the newspaper. Consider it done. Any particular reason we need to find her?"

"Yes, but I can't tell you right now. I promised."

"The plot thickens," he said. "I'll do my best."

"Thank you," she said. "Anything you can find out, particularly about where she is now, would be extremely helpful. But don't let Ed Johnson know that you're looking; the man is a pit bull."

"I'll call you as soon as I know something," he said.

He reached forward and pulled her into a quick hug. He was warm and solid and smelled faintly of an expensive men's cologne. Brenna resisted the urge to burrow against him. Barely.

"Have fun tonight but not too much," he growled in her ear, and she shivered. She watched the door swing shut behind him.

Brenna spent the rest of the day working on the dresser and thinking about Tenley having a baby and the half sibling she didn't even know she had.

Several of her leaf-peeping students stopped in.

Dan and Jan came to collect their tray and say good-bye.

Today they were wearing matching brown rag wool cardigans that Brenna recognized from a shop in town. Despite finding the body in the woods, they assured her that Morse Point was a lovely town.

Julie and Suede popped in as well. Suede mumbled something that sounded like a thank-you, and Julie sighed.

"This, too, shall pass," she said. "Or at least that's what my mother keeps telling me."

She picked up her tray and was quite pleased with how it had turned out. Brenna wanted to ask her about Dom, if she was going to see him again, but she knew it was none of her business. And asking Julie about her relationship with Dom wouldn't help Brenna sort out her own feelings about him. In fact, it would probably just confuse her more.

She watched as the mother and son made their way across the green. Julie leaned over to say something to Suede, and it must have been good, because he reached out and gave her a quick hug before resuming his slouching walk.

In thirteen years, that would be Tenley. Brenna couldn't believe it. Her best friend was going to be a mom. What a lucky baby to have Tenley and Matt for parents. The thought of it filled her with happiness. She'd have to think of something really special to decoupage for the baby.

In the meantime, she turned back to her dresser. She was gluing a paper vine from the bottom right corner of the lowest drawer up and across the next two drawers at an angle that would end in the upper left corner. She loved how the dark brown twisting vine stood out against the green background. The vine was so delicate, however, that it took steady hands and tremendous patience to place it just right.

She was dabbing excess glue off the middle drawer with a clean damp rag when Paula arrived to pick up her tray.

"Hi, Brenna. I hope I'm not interrupting," she said.

"Not at all; the rest of the tour group has come and gone," she said.

Paula examined Brenna's work. "That is lovely."

"Thanks," Brenna said. "I like working with my hands. It helps me think."

"About what?"

"Everything, I guess," she said. "Presently, about who killed Harvey Lester and what to wear on my date tonight."

"Ah, so you're multitasking," Paula said with a grin. She walked over to the shelf at the back of the shop and retrieved her tray. "Shouldn't you leave the murder investigation to the police?"

"Believe it or not, you're not the first person to ask me that," Brenna said. "I would. I mean I know Chief Barker will figure it out, but . . ."

"But?" Paula prompted.

"Tenley is very worried about her father, and I promised I'd do what I could to help," she said. "I just think if we can answer some questions about the past, we'll be able to resolve the present."

Paula studied her for moment as if she were trying to decide what to say. Finally, she said, "I can't help you with the murder, but I'm pretty good with fashion." She flushed and then gestured at herself in her khaki pants and blue sweater. "Not for me, of course; I'm a plain Jane, but I read all of the fashion magazines, and I've been told I have a pretty good eye."

"Okay, I'm game," Brenna said. "At this point, frankly, all advice is welcome."

"So, who is the man and how much do you like him?"

"He is my landlord, and I like him very much."

"Did he give you any idea about where you are going?"

"No, but he's picking me up at seven, so I'm assuming dinner," she said.

"It's going to be cold tonight," Paula said. "Do you own any sweaters that are sexy and warm?"

Brenna did a mental perusal of her closet. "I do have a Donna Karan belted sweater dress in black."

"Black is always safe," Paula said. "It can either dress up or dress down. Put out two pairs of shoes, and then when he picks you up and you see what he's wearing, you'll know if it's a low-heeled boot or a stiletto evening."

"Good thinking," Brenna said. "I'm so glad you stopped in; otherwise he'd probably find me in my bathrobe still deciding."

"That could work, too," Paula said with a giggle. She tucked a stray lock of blond hair behind her ear. "It was nice meeting you and Tenley. If I'm ever in Morse Point again, I'll be sure to look you up."

"Please do," Brenna said. She wiped off her sticky fingers on a paper towel and gave Paula a quick hug.

Paula hugged her back and then left the shop with her tray tucked under her arm. Brenna glanced at the window and noticed it was getting dark. If she was going to get ready for her date, she'd better close up and get moving.

Brenna rushed around her cabin, trying to get dressed, but it seemed as if everything was working against her. Maybe it was nerves, but she dropped her mascara wand and got brown-black goo all over her vanity table. Then she pulled on a pair of black tights to wear under her dress and discovered a run. Argh.

She was just fishing a new pair out of her dresser when the phone rang. She hurried over to her purse and snatched her cell phone out.

The number was Dom's. Maybe he had some information for her. She flipped it open. "Hi, Dom. Hold on just one second, okay?"

"Sure," he said.

Brenna put the phone down and quickly pulled on the black stockings. She shimmied them into place and then pulled her black dress down over them. A quick glance in the mirror told her she was ready all except for her shoes.

"I'm back," she said.

"What were you doing?" he asked. "It sounded like an aerobic workout."

"Pulling on my stockings," she said.

He heaved a sigh. "I'm going to try not to picture that. It's entirely too distracting."

Brenna felt her face grow warm. She tried to ignore it and asked, "Any news?"

"Some," he said. "One of my reporters from the *Morse Point Courier* was able to track down a Lynette Compton in New York State."

"Really?" Brenna gasped. "Is there any contact information?"

"Well, that's the interesting part," he said.

A knock sounded and Brenna said, "I'm sorry, Dom; someone is at the door."

"It must be the hot date," he said.

Brenna glanced at the clock on the kitchen wall. It was only six thirty. "If it is, he's very early."

"He must be eager," he said.

"I'm going to let that go," she said.

"It's fine. Put me on speaker," he said. "I'll talk while you walk."

Brenna hit the button on her cell that made it go into speaker mode and put it on the counter. "All right, but behave yourself. What do you know?"

"There is no contact information for Lynette Compton, since she died two years ago."

"Oh, no," Brenna said.

She glanced through the peephole and saw the back of a blond head on her porch. What was Tenley doing here? Maybe she thought Brenna needed help with prepping for her date. She unlocked the door and pulled it wide.

The head spun around and she found herself looking at Paula Marchesi.

"I know that's not helpful," Dom continued. "But there is some hope. Lynette had a child, a daughter named Paula."

Brenna opened her mouth to speak but no sound came out. Paula gave her a lopsided smile and stepped into the cabin. She picked up the phone and snapped it shut.

"Did I hear him say 'Paula'?" she asked. "So, I gather you just found out all about little old me, didn't you?"

CHAPTER 21

Shock left Brenna incapable of forming an answer. She stared stupidly at the young woman before her while Paula paced around the small cabin.

"I was planning on leaving town tonight," Paula said. "My work here was done, but no, you had to go and start digging. What was it you said? 'If we can answer some questions about the past, we'll be able to resolve the present'? Yeah, well, that sort of changed my plans."

"I'm not following you," Brenna said.

"Yes, you are," Paula said, and she pulled a small lethal-looking handgun out of her coat pocket.

"Easy," Brenna said. A whoosh of blood roared into her ears, making her own heart-beat echo in her head.

She looked Paula over. She was shorter than Brenna. She was also younger and probably faster. Could Brenna take her?

"I'll shoot you before you get a hand on me," Paula said. "I'm trained in firearms, and as you know from my previous work, I'm not afraid to use them."

"Previous work?" Brenna asked.

"Don't play dumb. Put on some shoes and let's go," Paula said. "Nice dress, by the way. Too bad the landlord lover will never get to see it."

Brenna's hands were shaking, and she grabbed the first pair of shoes she could find, her hiking boots by the back door. She also grabbed her coat.

"Where are we going?" she asked.

"You'll see," Paula said.

Brenna's phone began to ring. She was sure it was Dom calling back; if she could just grab it and cry for help, she might get out of this.

Paula took it and shoved it in a drawer, muting its ringtone. Brenna noticed she was wearing gloves. This did nothing to calm her galloping heart.

"Out." Paula gestured with the gun toward the door.

Brenna glanced at the clock. It was twenty minutes until her date. If she could just stall, maybe Nate would see them. She fumbled with the doorknob and got a painful shove in her right shoulder blade.

"I am well aware of the time," Paula said. "Now move."

She pushed Brenna past Siobhan's cabin — no lights were on inside — and onto the trail that led into the woods. It was dark, and Brenna had to pick her way in the gloom on the uneven ground over unearthed roots and deep pockets made by puddles. She could hear Paula breathing heavily behind her, and as the trees enveloped them in their twilight embrace, she was sure she had never heard a more terrifying sound.

After two years of hiking here, Brenna knew these woods well. She figured they were about a half mile out when Paula told her to stop.

A lesser-used trail, barely visible in the darkness, veered off to the right, and Paula pushed Brenna onto it, as if using her as a shield against the twiggy branches that jutted out, scratching her face and tearing her stockings.

They reached a clearing where a silver compact car was parked. Brenna hoped they had stumbled upon a couple in the midst of a tryst, anything to stop this madness. But no, Paula shoved her against the car and then unlocked it and yanked open the back door.

Out fell Siobhan with her hands and feet

bound by rope and a wide strip of tape over her mouth. Brenna glanced from her to Paula and back.

Paula laughed, but it wasn't a happy sound. It was a creepy chortle that made the hair on the nape of Brenna's neck twitch in alarm.

"You thought she was the killer, didn't you?" Paula asked. She reached down and hauled Siobhan to her feet.

Even in the dark, Brenna could see the pallor of Siobhan's skin, giving her a ghostly appearance. She glanced over her body, trying to see if she was hurt. She couldn't see any visible signs of injury, but her brown bob looked lank and stringy, and her jeans and white blouse were wrinkled and grubby.

"You're not the only one who snoops too much," Paula said. She bent down, and using a knife she'd taken from her coat pocket, she cut the rope off of Siobhan's ankles. "This one has been trying to be my friend for days. As if. With my upbringing, I can smell a pencil-pushing bureaucrat at ten yards."

"I don't understand," Brenna said, although she was afraid she did.

Paula ripped the tape off of Siobhan's mouth and said, "Explain it to her. I'd love to hear your take."

Siobhan gasped for breath. She inhaled the cold night air as if her lungs had been denied a deep breath for far too long.

She sagged a little and then looked at Brenna with eyes that were full of regret. "She killed Harvey Lester."

Brenna looked at Paula and asked, "Why?"

"Tell her," Paula ordered.

Siobhan licked her lips as if trying to give herself a moment. "As far as I have been able to determine, she and Mr. Lester planned to run away together, but he backed out at the last moment, so she killed him."

"Ms. Dwyer, here, is not the artist she pretends to be," Paula said.

"I know," Brenna said.

"Oh, really?" Paula asked. "How did you figure that out?"

Brenna could have bitten her tongue in half. If she stood any chance of getting out of this, she needed to keep her wits about her and her mouth shut.

"Come on, don't be shy," Paula said. Her voice was patronizing in its encouragement, like a teacher who flatters a student into admitting to bad behavior.

"The hatching marks on the work in her cabin are those of a left-handed artist, and she is right-handed," she said.

Siobhan's eyes widened and then narrowed. "I knew you were in my cabin."

"Sorry," Brenna said. "You left the door unlocked."

"So? That doesn't mean that you can come in uninvited," she said.

Paula glanced between them. Brenna could see by the manic light in her eye that she was enjoying their tiff. She wondered if that might be the ticket to get them out of this.

"Listen, if you would stick to one man and not try to latch onto every man that comes within reach, maybe other women would trust you a little bit more."

"What is that supposed to mean?" Siobhan snapped, looking offended.

"You've been trying to get your hooks into Nate all week," Brenna said. "Do you think I didn't notice?"

"Ooh, this is getting good," Paula said and turned to look at Siobhan.

Brenna took the opportunity to give Siobhan a wide-eyed stare over Paula's shoulder, hoping that she would catch on to her plan.

Siobhan's eyes narrowed and she growled, "Look, it's not my fault if you can't get Nate interested in you. You couldn't get Brian interested in you, either, and I know you tried."

Brenna sucked in a gasp of hurt, which was not all for show, and Paula looked at her with amused eyes and said, "She fights mean."

Siobhan widened her eyes at Brenna, letting her know she was following along.

"How do you know Brian wasn't interested?" Brenna challenged, taking a step closer to Siobhan.

"Because he told me so," she retorted, taking a step closer, too.

"Oh, yeah?" Brenna asked. This was her chance. Siobhan was standing within striking range. If she pretended to punch Siobhan, she could hit Paula instead, and they might be able to take her.

She balled up her fist but as she went to swing, something plowed into the backs of her knees and she went down with a thump on the hard, cold ground.

Paula leaned over Brenna and *tsk*ed. "Temper, temper."

Keeping her gun trained on the two of them, Paula reached into the car and pulled out a length of rope. Yanking Brenna up by the elbow, she tied her wrists behind her back just like Siobhan's. Brenna felt her stomach drop. She had no idea how they were going to get out of this now.

"Much as I've enjoyed this little show,"

she said, "we need to get going. I have a plane to catch."

"Plane?" Brenna asked.

"Yep," she said. "I've gotten all that I need from here and I'm good to go."

"Where are you going?" Siobhan asked.

"Yes, I'm sure the FBI would love to know where I'm headed, but I'm not about to tell you."

"You're FBI?" Brenna asked.

"And so is her boyfriend, Brian," Paula said. "He's the last item on my agenda."

"He doesn't know anything," Siobhan said quickly. "I never got a chance to tell him what I discovered."

"Oh, that's too bad," Paula said. "I still have to kill him, of course."

"Please don't," Siobhan said.

Brenna saw the pleading look on her face and felt badly for all of the not-so-nice things she'd thought about her. The fact that she was a federal agent did explain her incredible lack of people skills. Brenna imagined that in Siobhan's world, everyone was guilty until proven innocent.

"Oh, how touching — you're in love with your partner," Paula said. She shoved them toward the woods. Obviously, they were going to be taking a hike from which they wouldn't be coming back. "Too bad, so sad."

"You stole Tenley's ring," Brenna said.

She wasn't sure why she brought it up, but it just clicked in her brain, and it seemed like a good idea to keep Paula talking and distracted.

"You mean I took what should have been mine," Paula said. Her voice was brittle with bitterness. "I grew up in a crappy apartment with a drunk. There were no fancy houses or cars, servants, or prestigious schools for me. The very least I deserved was a family heirloom, don't you think?"

"Her father gave her that ring," Brenna said. "It meant the world to her."

"*Our* father gave her that ring. It should have been mine. All of it should have been mine. Instead, I was sent off to live in poverty with a woman who drank all day and puked all night, and when she got really bad, the caseworkers came and took me away, so I could go live in neglect and squalor elsewhere, but in a few months I was always returned. Did my father ever check on me? Did my father care about what happened to me? No. Rupert Morse couldn't let his perfect life be tarnished by the likes of me."

"I'm sure he cared," Brenna protested.

Paula gave a bark of laughter that cut through the night with a serrated edge. "Please, don't bother."

"If you kill us while Morse is in jail, they'll know he didn't kill Lester and he'll be let out," Siobhan said. "Then you won't have your precious revenge."

"That's only if they find your bodies," Paula said. "But I'm very confident that they won't."

CHAPTER 22

Brenna's teeth began to chatter and it wasn't from the cold. They traipsed through the woods, Brenna and Siobhan moving more slowly than normal. Perhaps it was an unconscious way to stall their impending deaths, or maybe it was just a lot harder to keep your balance with your hands behind your back.

Brenna wondered what Nate would do when she wasn't at the cabin. Would he think he'd been stood up? And what about Dom? Would he think her cell phone cut out or that she hung up on him?

She glanced at Siobhan. She could just make out her profile in the gloom. Was she thinking about Brian?

"So, you're FBI," Brenna said. "What brought you here?"

"Suspected money laundering," Siobhan said. "Huge sums of money were being passed through Lester and Morse to a bank account in New York. We were following the money. Brian got a job working there, and I came to town to see if I could cozy up to Lester."

"That's my bank account," Paula said. She stepped a little closer and leaned in. "I had Harvey socking away money for me."

"You made an error," Siobhan said. "Anything over ten thousand dollars in cash, and the banks are required to report it. The feds can freeze your account in a heartbeat, and if I go missing, they probably will."

Paula pushed her lower lip out in a small pout. Brenna marveled that she had ever been charmed by this girl.

"It's okay," Paula said. "I've been moving the money overseas. Even if they freeze my New York account, the bulk of it is already far away just waiting for me."

"So, why did you kill Lester?" Brenna asked. "Couldn't you just take the money and go without killing him?"

Siobhan tripped over a root and stumbled, falling to the ground. Paula let out an impatient sigh.

"Get up!" she snapped.

Siobhan rolled to her side and then onto her knees. Being locked in the car had obviously left her weak, and she moved slowly as she got back to her feet.

"Be more careful," Paula said. "I'd hate to have to shoot you before we get there."

"Where?" Siobhan asked.

"You'll see," Paula said. Her voice had a child-like singsong quality to it that made Brenna's skin crawl.

"To answer your question, Brenna, I had to kill Lester because he figured it out."

"Figured what out?" Brenna asked.

"That I'm Rupert Morse's daughter," she said. "My original plan had been to bankrupt the company by romancing a fortune out of Lester. That was going quite well until his wife caught on that he was cheating. Stupid man. He told her that he was in love with me and that we were soul mates — how embarrassing — and that we were going to run away together."

"You never planned to be with him, did you?"

"That old prune?" Paula gave a derisive laugh. "No way. But Mrs. Lester went to Morse and told him what Harvey was planning. He then told Harvey all about his affair with my mother. His argument was that affairs happen, but you don't throw your life away on them.

"Sadly, I hadn't counted on this. Most unfortunate for poor Harvey, he put it all together and realized I was Morse's daughter and that I wasn't in love with him, shocker, but was just using him to destroy Morse."

"So, you shot him," Siobhan said. Her head was cocked to the side as she walked, and Brenna could tell she was cataloging every word Paula said.

"What choice did I have?" Paula snapped. "He actually wanted all of the money back. I mean, really, like that was going to happen."

Leaves crunched and twigs snapped under their feet. The night air was cold and Brenna could see her breath. Despite her familiarity with the woods, she was struggling to figure out where they were or how they could get out of here.

"Stop here," Paula ordered.

Siobhan and Brenna both stopped and turned to face her.

"It worked out better than I hoped," Paula said. "Daddy dearest will now spend his life in jail and I will be free. Free to live the life I always deserved."

"No one has the right to take a life," Siobhan said, stepping toward Paula.

"They took my life first," Paula said and shoved Siobhan back.

Siobhan staggered and fell against Brenna, who felt something sharp gouge her wrists.

Siobhan was stabbing at the rope with what felt like a piece of glass. She must have picked it up when she'd fallen.

Brenna didn't even care if Siobahn nicked her skin. She pulled against the rope and felt the glass slice it, leaving it frayed. She knew it would be enough. She shoved Siobhan away as if she was annoyed.

Paula was watching them through a narrowed gaze.

"Just because you had a rough childhood is no reason to murder people to get what you want," Brenna said. She wanted to distract her from watching Siobhan too closely.

"What do you know?" Paula snapped. "I know all about you, Brenna Miller. You grew up in Boston, attended private schools, and lived a privileged life. Until you decided to rob your own art gallery, and then it all went wrong, didn't it?"

Brenna felt her teeth clench. "I didn't rob the gallery."

"Yeah, sure," Paula scoffed. "Then why are you hiding out in this backwoods town? What happened? Did your criminal friends screw you over?"

Brenna felt a hot burst of rage override her panic. She welcomed it. It felt so much better than being afraid.

"You don't know anything," she snapped. "Certainly not about me. I came here to get away from the criminals in Boston, the ones who stripped me of my life there, but what I have come to discover is that bad people are everywhere, and they are frequently the people you least suspect."

"Is that a jab at me?" Paula asked. "Did I disappoint you? Pardon me if I couldn't care less."

Brenna opened her mouth to retort but Siobhan made a sudden leap at Paula. She'd gotten her hands free, and the two of them went down with a grunt and an oomph.

Brenna scrambled to rip off the rope at her wrists. She yanked her arms apart and the rope gave way, freeing her hands. She was shaking off the rope when a gunshot roared through the night air, and she jumped with a screech.

"Siobhan, are you all right?" she called.

"I've got her gun," Siobhan said. "Run, Brenna, run!"

The two women thrashed on the ground. Brenna tried to get closer, but in the night-time shadows, she couldn't see who was who. Something sailed passed Brenna's head, and with a curse, Paula jumped off of Siobhan.

"Damn it, Brenna, run!" Siobhan yelled.

She was holding her shoulder with one hand, and even in the dark, Brenna could see the bloody stain spreading on her white blouse.

"Go! Now!" Siobhan ordered.

Paula was thrashing around in the leaves, searching for her weapon. Brenna knew the only chance Siobhan had was for her to run and get help. Paula would have to chase her since she couldn't risk Brenna bringing help. Brenna just hoped she could outrun Paula and get back to Siobhan in time. Without looking back, she tore through the woods.

Branches reached out and clawed at her. She twisted her ankles on roots and rocks and still she ran. She could hear Paula pounding the earth behind her, swearing at her, cursing her, and still Brenna ran. A gunshot went off and a tree to Brenna's right exploded in a shower of wood and bark. Apparently, Paula had found her gun.

Terrified, Brenna put on a burst of speed. Her lungs were burning from the cold night air, and she ducked between the large tree trunks, hoping for cover. She saw the wink of a light through the trees and she knew she was getting closer to the cabins. The sound of the lake lapping against the shore filled the night, and she broke through the trees back onto the main path.

There was a grunt behind her and she knew that Paula had either fallen or run into a tree. Brenna dashed on, hoping to buy herself some time.

The porch lights from all of the cabins were on, illuminating the little community of cabins around the lake. She ran toward them, cutting across the meadow.

A lone figure was running toward her. Brenna recognized him instantly and felt her heart lift. Of course, he was here just when she needed him most. She almost burst into tears, she was so relieved to see him.

"Brenna!" he called. She plowed into him, and he hugged her close.

"Are you all right? Where have you been? I was getting worried," he said. He was running his hands over her, as if assuring himself that she was all right.

"There's no time." Brenna glanced over her shoulder. "She's coming and she has a gun."

She grabbed his hand and began to run toward the cabins. They skirted around the corner of the second vacant one. She glanced up and saw Chief Barker's squad car cruising down the driveway.

"Chief Barker's here?"

"He was. He's just leaving," he said. "He got a call about a missing person and came out here to check."

"Siobhan," Brenna said. Brian must have called about her. She wondered how long Siobhan had been in that car and how much longer she could lie bleeding in the woods. A sob escaped her.

"Brenna, who are we hiding from?" he asked. "What's happening?"

"Paula, one of my leaf-peeping students, showed up at my cabin. She had a gun. She shot Siobhan."

"What?" He pulled Brenna around to face him. He cupped her face, and even in the faint light from the distant cabins, she could see the intensity of his gaze as it met hers.

"I'm fine," Brenna said and squeezed his hands in reassurance. She turned back to the corner of the cabin to peer at the woods. Sure enough, Paula came tumbling through the trees. She was gasping for breath and brandishing her gun.

"Brenna, come out, come out, wherever you are." Paula's voice was singsong and sickeningly sweet and made Brenna's scalp prickle with alarm.

A sweep of headlights shone across the grass as a car pulled into the lot.

"Oh, thank goodness, the chief is back,"

Brenna said. But when they glanced up at the communal parking lot, it wasn't Chief Barker; it was Tenley and Matt.

"Oh, no," Brenna said. "I have to go and head them off. She'll shoot Tenley for sure."

"Why would she shoot Tenley?" he asked.

"Because Tenley is her half sister," Brenna said. "Stay here."

"No, I'll go; you stay," he said.

But it was too late. Paula had already seen Tenley. She strode across the grass, determination in her steps. In the gloom, Brenna could see the similarity between them. They had the same posture and tilt to their noses; even their chins jutted in the same stubborn manner. But where Tenley's face was soft with kindness and warmth, Paula's was brittle with bitterness and resentment. Why hadn't Brenna seen it before?

"Paula!" Tenley cried, sounding happy to see the girl of whom she'd grown so fond. "I thought you had left to go back to New York."

"Change of plans," Paula said. Her eyes were scanning the dark as she held the gun behind her back.

"Oh, well, if you're staying, you'll have to come to the next decoupage class," Tenley said. "I'm sure Brenna has something wonderful planned."

"I'll mark my calendar," she said. "Speaking of Brenna, have you talked to her lately?"

"No, in fact, she was supposed to call me earlier, but she never did," Tenley said. "I suppose I'm being overprotective, but I had a bad feeling and we were on our way past, so we thought we'd pop in to see if she was here."

"I thought she said something about having a date," Paula said.

"See? I told you," Matt said. "She's out on a hot date. I'm sure she'll call you later and tell you all about it in glorious detail."

Brenna could feel the man pressed up against her back. The heat of him was so warm and reassuring, she wasn't even embarrassed that they were listening to others discuss her love life.

Please go, she thought, hoping Tenley would get her mental message. *Go, go, go.*

"Do you think she'll harm them?" he whispered in her ear.

"I don't know," Brenna said. "I hope not. Oh, God, I hope not."

"Stay here," he said.

"But what are you . . . ?" She didn't get a chance to finish the question.

Nate's lips landed on hers in a kiss that was firm and swift, as if he were trying to memorize the feel of her against him and at the same time promising her that he'd be right back. And then he was gone.

Brenna clamped her hand to her mouth as he slipped around the back side of the cabin. What was he going to do? This couldn't be good.

She refused to let Nate put himself in danger. She carefully crept to the front corner of the cabin. Her heart was hammering in her throat.

"Are you ready, Tenley?" Matt asked.

"I guess so," Tenley said, although she didn't sound very sure.

She turned to go, but then spun back around and stared at Paula. "I'm sorry; why did you say you were here?"

CHAPTER 23

There was a moment of taut silence as the two women stared at each other. Then Paula tossed her hair back and gave Tenley a slow smile.

"I came by looking for Brenna, but I must have missed her. I had a decoupage question for her, but I only just remembered about her date. I was just admiring the beautiful lake."

"Oh," Tenley said. She looked somewhat reassured.

Brenna felt herself relax as Matt took her arm and led her away. Paula's gaze whipped to the cabins, and Brenna knew she was searching for her.

She couldn't very well shoot Brenna with Matt and Tenley in earshot, but Brenna didn't want to do anything that would endanger them or the baby, so she waited until they reached their car.

Brenna stepped forward. Paula spun to

face her. They stared at each other for the briefest moment when all of a sudden a shadow erupted from behind the other side of the cabin and launched itself at Paula. She went down with a shriek.

Hank had caught her off guard and toppled her. Nate was right behind him, and Brenna ran forward. Paula still had the gun and Brenna was not about to let anything happen to the two most important men in her life.

Brenna saw Paula trying to get her gun hand free to shoot. Before she could, Brenna lifted her right leg and stomped on Paula's wrist, trapping it under her heavy boot. Then she reached down and wrenched the gun out of Paula's hand.

With the loss of her weapon, it was easy for Nate to subdue Paula. He stood up and hauled her with him. Matt and Tenley came racing back.

"Brenna!" Tenley cried. "What's going on? Are you holding a gun?"

"Call Chief Barker," Brenna said. She held the gun loosely at her side, facing away from them as if it were a bomb that might go off on its own. "Siobhan's been shot. She needs an ambulance."

Matt immediately fished his phone out of his pocket and dialed the chief's number.

"Let me go!" Paula tried to yank her arms out of Nate's strong hands. "You have no right to hold me."

"You killed Harvey Lester," Brenna said. "We have every right to keep you here until the chief arrives."

"What?" Tenley asked. Her eyes went wide. "Paula killed Uncle Harvey? But why?"

"Why do you think, Sis?" Paula snapped.

"What did you call me?" Tenley looked at Paula as if she'd sprouted another head.

Paula's eyes narrowed with cruelty. "You heard me, Sister dearest. Why don't you ask Daddy who I am? Then again, he paid my mother off to disappear while she was pregnant with me, so maybe he doesn't remember having a torrid affair with his secretary twenty-four years ago."

Tenley's eyes were huge and she wobbled on her feet. Matt closed his phone and reached out to steady her with an arm.

"That's not true," Tenley said. "You're lying. My father would never do anything like that."

Paula gave a bitter laugh. "Would and did, sweetie. Can't you see the resemblance between us? I've been studying us. We both have his nose and chin and his blue eyes."

Tenley looked from Paula to Brenna. "Tell

me she's crazy. Tell me this isn't true."

"I'm sorry, Tenley," Brenna said. "You're only half-right. She is crazy, but I'm afraid it is true. Your father did have an affair, and it did produce a child."

"Let me go and I won't tell," Paula bargained. "Let me go and I'll give your ring back."

"You took my ring?"

"It should be mine," Paula said, sounding petulant. "But I'll give it back; just let me go."

"I'm afraid not," Nate said. He glanced at Brenna and she nodded. He began to lead Paula up to the parking lot.

Several cars with flashing blue and red lights arrived and illuminated them where they stood. Nate had to half drag, half carry Paula as she fought his hold. She punched at him with her free hand, but he pushed her relentlessly forward.

"Stop!" Paula screeched. "No! You've ruined everything. Everything!"

Brenna walked over to Tenley and enfolded her in a hug while Chief Barker handcuffed Paula and put her in the back of one of the squad cars. Officer Meyers stayed with her while Chief Barker and Officer DeFalco came running across the lawn with Brian Steele and two EMTs on his heels.

"Where is she?" Brian looked wildly at the group. "Where's Siobhan?"

"She's in the woods," Brenna said. "She was shot in the shoulder."

"Brenna, do you think you can lead us to her?" Chief Barker asked.

"I think so," she said. She squeezed Tenley's arm, took a deep breath, and ran back into the woods. She fervently hoped they weren't too late.

The beams of several flashlights illuminated the path and it was nowhere near as scary as it had been the last time, but still Brenna felt her heart pounding heavily in her chest. This time she wasn't running for her life, however; this time she was running for someone else's. They had to find Siobhan and quickly.

Just when she was sure she must have taken a wrong turn and lost her way, she saw her, a splotch of white in the dark woods.

"This way," she cried. The heavy tread of booted feet sounded behind her as they pounded down the seldom-used trail. "Siobhan, we're coming!"

She saw Siobhan raise her hand to signal that she'd heard. Brenna let the men run around her to get to her. Brian crouched at her side and held her hand while the EMTs went to work with improvised lighting provided by Chief Barker and Officer De-Falco.

Brenna stepped forward and looked down on Siobhan in the glare of the large Maglites. Her eyes were shut and her skin was so pale it was almost translucent. The EMTs were trying to get a line into her arm and Brian was whispering softly to her.

"Brenna, I want you to tell me everything you know," the chief said.

Brenna talked while they worked. She told them everything about Paula and her affair with Harvey; her revenge on her father, Rupert Morse; and how she shot Siobhan. Finally, she wound down.

"And then Hank jumped on her and Nate subdued her while I got her gun," Brenna said. She glanced down and realized she was still holding the weapon. "Here."

She handed the gun to the chief, who checked that the safety was on and then tucked it into his belt.

Having told him everything she knew, she took a deep, restorative breath. The chief let out a low whistle, which Brenna took to mean he hadn't seen this mess coming. She knew exactly how he felt.

"All right, she's stable, but we need to get her to the hospital ASAP," one of the paramedics said.

They each took one end of the stretcher and began the long hike back to the cabins and the ambulance. Chief Barker and Officer DeFalco lit the way and Brenna followed. The trip back seemed faster, and before she knew it, they were striding across the meadow toward the waiting ambulance.

As they got ready to load her, Siobhan glanced up at Brenna and gave her a small smile. "Thanks."

"You're welcome." Brenna stepped back, and Brian hopped into the back with one of the paramedics, and the doors slammed shut. With a flash of lights, they tore off down the driveway.

Brenna scanned the small crowd that had formed until she spotted Nate. He stepped up beside her and put his arm around her shoulder. She was shaky with spent nerves, and she turned into his arms, seeking warmth and comfort.

"Brenna, can you come down to the station?" Chief Barker asked.

She nodded and heard Nate say, "I'll drive her in."

The chief tipped his head and turned to the squad car where Paula was sitting, cuffed. He banged twice on the roof and Officer Meyers turned on the engine. Paula's face was a contorted mask of rage on the other side of the glass. She stared at Brenna with a malevolence that made her shudder.

DeFalco and the chief followed quickly in their cars. Brenna stood in the circle of Nate's arms and watched their taillights disappear down the drive, carrying Harvey Lester's murderer to jail.

CHAPTER 24

Brenna set out carrying two of Stan's tasty lattes across the town green, although it was really more of a town brown now that all the grass had died. A bitter wind from the north made her burrow her nose into her scarf, and she was grateful for the hot cups of coffee warming her hands.

The sky was a stern steel gray with clouds that held the threat of snow in them. It would be the first of the season, but that was okay. She had her fireplace all ready to go, and she even had someone to share it with. Life was good.

She had made it halfway across the square when she saw him. He was dressed casually in jeans and a thick wool sweater. As she watched, he took a vibrant orange Nerf football and threw a spiral pass across the park to a carrot-topped adolescent thirty yards away. Even from here, she could feel the raw power pulsing from him.

It had been a week since Paula's arrest, and although she had talked to Dom, she hadn't seen him. She had discovered that the reason Chief Barker had first shown up at the cabins was because Brian had called to report Siobhan missing, and then Dom had called the chief to report a disturbance at Brenna's cabin. Dom hadn't known that she was in danger; he'd just had a feeling that their phone call hadn't ended naturally and had badgered Chief Barker into going and checking on her.

Suede, the recipient of Dom's pass, caught the ball and sent it back in a less-practiced spiral. A woman with the same vibrant hair appeared, and just before Dom caught the ball, she ran in front of him and snatched it out of the air.

Dom didn't hesitate. He tackled her. Their laughter rang out in the crisp air and got even louder when Suede came charging up to tackle the man who had sacked his mom.

As the group broke apart, Dom glanced up and saw Brenna watching them. He grinned and she smiled back at him. She was glad he and Julie had found each other. They seemed to be a perfect fit.

She raised her paper cup at him in a silent salute, and he nodded his head. Brenna was happy for him and happy that there seemed to be no hard feelings that she had chosen Nate. She was confident that their friendship would stay intact; after all, she never knew when she was going to need the former mobster in her life.

She continued across the green and crossed the street. When she got to Vintage Papers, she hooked one arm through the handle on the door and pulled it open. The bells jangled and she slipped through the open door, letting it close behind her.

"Baby Mama," she called. "I've got your decaf latte."

A dark-haired woman was standing in the center of the shop with her back to Brenna. She slowly turned and Brenna almost dropped her lattes. It was Tricia Morse, Tenley's mother.

Brenna felt her jaw go slack. If ever there was a foot-in-mouth-ectomy needed, it was right now.

Tenley was standing just past her mother at the counter, and she smiled at what had to be a look of complete horror on Brenna's face.

"It's all right," she said. "She knows. Now give me my latte."

Brenna stretched out her hand and gave Tenley the cup with her latte.

"Good afternoon, Mrs. Morse. It's nice to

see you again."

Mrs. Morse looked her over. "Yes, I don't believe we've seen each other since that dressing-down you gave us over dessert."

"What did you do?" Tenley asked.

"I just gave them my point of view," Brenna said. She took a restorative sip of her coffee.

"It spoke well of you," Mrs. Morse said. "I'm glad Tenley has a friend like you."

"Thank you, Mrs. Morse. That's nice of you to say," Brenna said. She wondered briefly if she was dreaming. Mrs. Morse had never come into Tenley's shop before and in fact had been very vocal in her disapproval of her daughter going into a trade. What could she possibly be doing here today? Did she have a sudden need for paper goods?

"Call me Tricia," Mrs. Morse said. "Please."

"All right." Brenna pinched herself just to make sure she wasn't asleep. Ouch. Nope, not sleeping.

"Do you know why I never worked?" Tricia suddenly asked them.

"Because you had four daughters," Tenley said. "That is work."

"It was," Tricia agreed. "But not to me. I loved being a mother. I loved having these four beaming symbols of your father's love for me. It made me feel almost as if I was worthy of him."

Brenna and Tenley exchanged a look. Brenna nodded toward the back room. She didn't want to intrude on a mother-daughter moment, but Tenley shook her head, letting her know that she was to stay put.

"You were worthy of him, Mother," Tenley said. "More than worthy. When I think about what he did, I just . . ."

"I wasn't surprised when I found out," Tricia said. She was wearing a slim gray wool dress and black pumps. Her heels clicked against the wood floor as she strolled over to a display rack to examine some papers. "I always knew he would stray one day. How could he not? He was so handsome and I . . . Well . . ."

"Just because he was handsome, that's no reason for him to cheat on his wife," Tenley said. "And he didn't just hurt you; look at the poor woman who was cast aside and her child, my sister. Look at the damage that was done to them."

Tenley's voice rose and Brenna felt really uncomfortable and wished she hadn't hurried back from Stan's quite so quickly.

"Don't judge your father too harshly," Tricia said. "It was my fault. What happened to that woman and her daughter was my fault."

"Your fault?" Tenley repeated. "How?"

"I loved him so much, I was so afraid of losing him, that I . . ." Tricia's voice trailed off.

"You what?"

"I forced him to send them away," Tricia said. She spun back around to face them, and her face was filled with regret. "Maybe if I hadn't done that, Harvey would still be alive and that young woman wouldn't be in prison."

"Mom." Tenley put her coffee down and came around the counter. She wrapped her arms around her mother and said, "They made their own choices, Harvey to cheat on his wife and Paula to seek revenge. It could have been handled so differently by everyone; no one person is to blame."

Tricia Morse placed her hand alongside her daughter's face. "That is what has always made you special, your infinite capacity to love."

Okay, now Brenna definitely felt like she was intruding. She began to ease her way slowly back through the shop.

"Matt is very lucky to have you, you know," Tricia said.

"We're lucky to have each other," Tenley

corrected.

"Just so," Tricia said, and she kissed Tenley's head. Brenna felt a lump well up in her throat.

The bells on the door jangled again and Brenna paused. If it was a customer, she wanted to jump in so Tenley could have her time with her mother.

A tall, silver-haired man entered the shop. It was Tenley's father, looking more haggard than Brenna had ever seen him.

"Ready to go, Tricia?" he asked.

"Yes." Tricia gave Tenley one more quick squeeze, and she walked to the door. Mr. Morse held it open and she walked through, patting him on the arm as she went.

Mr. Morse turned to follow, but then he turned back to look at his daughter.

"You are the best of us; you know that, don't you?" he asked.

Tenley pressed her lips together, looking like she might cry.

"I'm very proud of you, Tenley," her father said as he glanced around the shop. "Very proud of you."

The door swung shut behind him, and Brenna watched as Mr. and Mrs. Morse walked down the street arm in arm, bracing against the wind. It was hard to say who was supporting whom, but maybe after so many years of marriage that was just the way of it.

It was late when Brenna arrived at her cabin from the shop. The purple cloak of twilight was just covering the trees, as if tucking their leafless limbs in for the night.

The evening air was brisk, and she hurried down the grass hill toward her little house, looking forward to a hot cup of tea. She wished she'd had the presence of mind this morning to prep something for dinner, because the thought of cooking a meal after such a long day in the shop did not appeal.

Her footsteps faltered as she noted that the light was on in her cabin. She was sure she hadn't left it on. She waited, expecting to feel the old, cold-fingered fist of dread clutch at her insides. That familiar nagging feeling of paranoia that had caused her to leave the hustle and bustle of Boston and move to Morse Point two years ago.

But amazingly, she didn't feel afraid. She felt merely curious. She thought she may have forgotten to lock her door and perhaps one of her neighbors had popped in to borrow something.

She renewed her walk toward the small house. It was remarkable, really, that she should feel no fear. After all, there had been murders in this little town, and yet she couldn't help but feel safe here. She wondered why.

And then the answer came as the front door to her cabin was pulled open and out charged a familiar golden coat of fur, Hank, followed by a tall man with a tousled head of brown hair and an intense pair of gray eyes. Nate.

This was why the fear had left her. She reached down and received Hank's slobbering licks and then stood as Nate pulled her into a crusher hug and planted a warm kiss on her lips that lingered.

"We missed you today," he said. "Come on, the game is about to start and I made a pot roast."

"Seriously?" she asked.

"Yeah," he said. "You're going to need to fortify yourself to withstand the Sox's defeat."

Brenna could have argued with him about whose team was going to lose, and judging by the twinkle in his eye, he was expecting as much. Instead, she placed her hand on the side of his face and whispered, "I love you."

His eyes scanned her face as if savoring the moment, and then he said, "I love you, too."

He tucked her under his arm, and Hank pressed against her other side. As the three of them made their way into her cabin, Brenna knew she was home.

DECOUPAGE PROJECTS

DECOUPAGE PUMPKIN
White glue or decoupage medium
Pumpkin
Cutout images of bats, spiders, or ghosts
Paintbrush

First apply a thin layer of decoupage medium on the pumpkin. Then position the cutout images on the pumpkin. Apply a thin layer of decoupage medium over the cutouts with the paintbrush. Carefully, with damp fingers or a cloth, smooth out any air bubbles that may have formed under the cutouts while applying the pictures. Let the pumpkin dry completely. Then apply another coat or two of decoupage medium, depending on the thickness of the images. Allow each layer of solution to dry completely before you apply the next.

DECOUPAGE TRAY

Wooden tray
Wood putty
Fine sandpaper
Paintbrushes
Acrylic primer
Acrylic paint
White glue or decoupage medium
Cutout images for decoupage
Polyurethane
Dry cloth
Self-adhesive felt circles

Clean the tray with hot soapy water and allow the tray to dry completely. Fill any scratches, dents, or holes with wood putty, and use fine sandpaper to sand the tray smooth. Apply a coat of acrylic primer. Set aside to dry. Apply two coats of acrylic paint in the color of your choice, allowing the tray to dry between coats. Once the second coat of paint has dried, spread a thin layer of decoupage medium on the tray and arrange the cutout images as you want them. Make sure there are no wrinkles or air bubbles. Set aside to dry thoroughly. Once dry, brush on two coats of polyurethane, allowing the tray to dry between applications. Use fine sandpaper to smooth the tray after the second coat of polyurethane dries, and wipe the tray with a dry cloth to remove any dust. Apply a final coat of polyurethane. Allow to dry completely. Affix a felt circle to each of the bottom corners to finish your decoupage tray.

Tip: To make your own decoupage solution, simply use equal amounts of plain white school glue and water. Mix until smooth and use as directed.